LUCY EDEN

My Friends and Myself

FRANCIS POULENC

MY FRIENDS AND MYSELF

Conversations assembled by
STÉPHANE AUDEL
Translated by
JAMES HARDING

London
DENNIS DOBSON

Copyright © 1963 by La Palatine, Geneva and Paris
English text copyright © 1978 by Dobson Books Ltd.
Originally published under the title *Moi et mes amis*
by Editions La Palatine, Paris
All rights reserved

First published in Great Britain in 1978
by Dobson Books Ltd., 80 Kensington Church Street, London W8
Printed by Clarke, Doble & Brendon Ltd, Plymouth and London
ISBN 0 234 77251 4

To the memory of
my niece
BRIGITTE MANCEAUX

Translator's Note

As in the French edition of this book, an attempt has been made to preserve the colloquialisms and minor digressions which arose out of the spontaneity of the original broadcast conversations and lent them their charm. Brief biographical details are added at the end of the book relating to figures who may not be familiar to every English reader.

J.H.

Contents

Preface—The last days at Noizay   13

I MY YOUTH

1. Paris and Nogent-sur-Marne   29
2. Studies: Koechlin and Viñes   34
3. Les Six and Diaghilev   39
4. Landowska, Bernac, Éluard and some songs   45
5. Apollinaire and Chabrier; Poulenc's secular works   51
6. Religious works; method of composing   56

II MY FRIENDS

1. Erik Satie   63
2. Max Jacob   72
3. Manuel de Falla   87
4. Paul Éluard   97
5. Arthur Honegger   106
6. Serge Prokofiev   114
7. Maurice Ravel   125
8. Igor Stravinsky   135

Personalia   145

Index   149

List of Illustrations

Francis Poulenc (M. T. Mabille) Frontispiece

Between pages 92 and 93

Francis Poulenc as a small boy
Schoenberg and Poulenc, Vienna, 1922
"Les Six"
Erik Satie in middle age
Stravinsky
Pierre Bernac and Francis Poulenc on their return from the USA, 1949
Suzanne Peignot, the favourite singer of his early songs, with Poulenc
Max Jacob and Lucien Daudet
Denise Duval in *Les Mamelles de Tirésias*
Paul Éluard, by Picasso
Léon-Paul Fargue, Maurice Ravel, Georges Auric, Paul Morand
Francis Poulenc at Noizay

Preface

THE LAST DAYS AT NOIZAY

The conversations which make up this book were broadcast by the Suisse-Romande Radio, whose kindness has made publication possible. The first six were given in 1953—which explains why there is no mention of works as important as *Le Dialogue des Carmélites* or *La Voix humaine*, since they were not yet written—and the remaining eight in 1955 and 1962. They were to be followed by four new broadcasts devoted to Diaghilev, Wanda Landowska, Schoenberg, Webern and Alban Berg, and, finally, opera. A recording session was arranged for the 30th January, 1963, the very day Francis Poulenc died. His sudden death put an end to a project which, with his usual care, he had prepared at the beginning of January in his house at Noizay in Touraine. How was I to guess, when I went there with him, that I should be the last of his friends to enjoy his lavish hospitality? This sad privilege brought with it, unfortunately, no consolation whatever.

For those who knew him well, the name of Francis Poulenc is bound up with "Le Grand Coteau", that lovely eighteenth-century house where everything is planned for comfort and pleasure. There he found the silence and calm favourable to his work. Built against a rocky mound pierced with deep troglodytic cellars, "Le Grand Coteau" has tall windows which open on to a terrace jutting out over a formal garden. Flanked on the right by an orangery which served as a dining-room in summer, and on the left by a clump of

My Friends and Myself

hundred-year-old lime trees dispensing shade and coolness on very hot days, it confronts a lower garden where there are vegetables, a vine that produces light golden wine, and—particularly—flowers, flowers in profusion.

The arrangement of the house inside revealed the owner's infallible taste. There was no piece of furniture, no picture or ornament which had not been chosen with care and placed in such a way as immediately to give an impression of perfection. Abundantly stocked with valuable books and rare editions, the library yielded nothing in size to a gramophone record collection whose variety testified to Poulenc's eclecticism. The spacious workroom, where an upright and a grand piano, loaded with photographs of his friends, stood next to each other, was adorned with a large fireplace. When evening fell, logs flamed and crackled happily there. Buried in an ample armchair, Francis followed with the score operas by Verdi and Puccini, symphonies by Mahler and Hindemith, concertos by Bartók, other music by Falla, Debussy, Chabrier (his beloved Chabrier), Mussorgsky, Stravinsky, Prokofiev, and the works of the Viennese twelve-note composers whose vocal and orchestral riches poured forth from the record-player. Thus he followed the unchanging timetable of his days. An orderly man if ever there was one, he arranged the books, scores, collections of autographs and photographs, and the letters he prized, with the same precision as he organized the hours given over to work.

Having risen early and eaten a breakfast of buttered rusks, jam and tea, Francis Poulenc would shut himself away in his workroom. Turning his back to the windows through which there flooded a stream of sunlight, he worked at his table or at his piano. From my room I could hear him thumping out chords, starting a phrase of music over again, altering it, wrestling with it tirelessly until a sudden silence indicated that he had returned to his table and was writing the notes

Preface

on his manuscript paper, or he was erasing those that didn't satisfy him with a scraping-knife whose blade had been shaped by wear to such an extent that it was reduced by half its size. This determined labour went on until lunch-time. Francis then went upstairs to his room, had a quick wash, and from that moment onwards devoted himself to the calls of friendship.

Dressed in a tweed jacket and flannel trousers, the complete "gentleman farmer" [sic], he would check that all the vases were filled with attractive bunches of flowers. He arranged them himself with an art that the most accomplished florist would have envied. I can see him again, one glorious September day, wearing a Panama hat, armed with a sunshade and carrying a long basket in which there lay a pair of secateurs.

"Let's go down to the lower garden," he suggested, "I'll cut the gladioli and the roses, but don't forget to hold the sunshade over my head. There's always the danger of sunstroke, not to mention those summer colds—they can be terrible, terrible!" For he took great care of his health and believed in the joint virtues of allopathy, homeopathy, osteopathy, acupuncture, and all the other medical treatments imaginable.

Sometimes he would find that an "extremely urgent" errand called him to the village. He would go into the depths of one of those troglodytic cellars where you could have garaged three large cars with ease, but where, in fact, there were only casks of wine and . . . a Solex scooter. He would get astride it, after swopping his Panama for a cap which he put on his head with the peak back to front so that it would protect his neck: "Like Blériot!" he used to say, laughing. And nothing was more amusing than the sight of this impressively tall, ruddy-complexioned man, his snuffly nose catching every scent and his mischievous eye noting the smallest detail of the landscape, as he whirled off amid the purring of the engine and a cloud of white dust towards the village where he always met with a unanimous welcome. When he was on his own at Noizay he never failed to make up a hand at cards in the company of the local innkeeper, the chauffeur and the carpenter, people with whom he was quite as at ease as in the drawing-rooms of the Princesse de Polignac or the Vicomtesse de Noailles. At home in princely mansions, a guest in the houses of international society, he would sometimes spend whole weeks in a monk-like room in the country and think himself very lucky, provided he was allowed to have a piano.

"I only like the aristocracy and the common people", he confessed to me one day. He might have added, "and my friends", but they occupied such an obvious place in his affections that he never even mentioned it.

No friendship was more loyal, more constant than the friendship offered by this great egocentric. The moment it was granted it remained unshakeable. Wherever he might be, in spite of his work and the demands of fame, his gift for friendship showed itself. Whether he was in America, England, Italy or any other of the countries where performances of his music and his concerts took him, his friends had news of him. He never forgot them, told them about his plans, fretted over theirs, and invited them months in advance to lunch in his Paris flat where you could look out over the whole extent of the Luxembourg gardens. Letter writing was for him something of an overruling duty which he did not attempt to evade. He devoted his afternoons to it, though not before having done justice to the courses of a lunch that reached the succulent standards his enjoyment of good food demanded. On fine days one had one's coffee, and then tea, on the terrace, while one's glance wandered over the countryside and its harmonious lines, its various elements perfectly balanced with an accuracy you could describe as geometrical. There was never any question of going for walks. Poulenc had little taste for that

Preface

sort of thing. On the other hand, he delighted in naughty little stories, society tittle-tattle, back-stage gossip, and memories of travel. He questioned me countless times about South America, which I'd visited at length, although he didn't have the slightest wish to go there.

"I did a concert tour of North Africa not long ago," he declared. "That's quite exotic enough for me!"

He was wholly French and above all Parisian. When away from Paris, France or Italy, he felt he was in exile. Yet he was very fond of England and North America. There he found the unreserved approval his insecurity thirsted after. Subject to deep and sudden depressions, he fled from boredom and sought diversion. Absence made him vulnerable to everything that could hurt and wound him.

When he was reaching the end of work on La Voix humaine he wrote to me: "La Voix humaine is finished. Cocteau is delighted and the ladies are in tears. I shall orchestrate it quickly so as to get rid of the nightmare, for it's a work I've written in a veritable state of fear. What with Les Carmélites I've had enough of harrowing subjects." He added: "When shall I write happy music again?"

Happiness! It was, together with sadness, the basis of his character. His music is impregnated with it, even when you take into account the fervour, the devoutness which is shown in his religious music. Poulenc's faith had nothing in common with metaphysical anguish. It glowed within him with a gentle certainty, it was like a providential refuge which, for its beneficial effects, may be compared with the peaceful countryside of Touraine and its pearly light, or the gentle roll of its wooded hills where slate roofs twinkle in the sun.

"My faith is that of a country priest," he confessed; and no one knew it better than he did.

I associate him in my memory with summer mornings, with afternoons filled with the humming of insects, with golden twighlights when the Loire veiled itself in a light mist, with evenings when music reigned supreme, with that lovely house made for ease, rest, meditation and work.

But it was not in a Touraine such as I have just described that we met at the beginning of January. Cold froze the whole country in its grip. A low-lying sky heavy with snow lent a chilly sternness to houses where every opening was blocked up, and even to the village streets where no one dared venture. "Le Grand Coteau" seemed by comparison all the more welcoming. Francis Poulenc was there to finish correcting the proofs of his *Répons des ténèbres* and to draw up the plan of the four conversations to which I have already referred. I had never seen him in such a happy mood nor readier for work. Scarcely had I moved into my room than he lent me books about the Russian Ballet and the Viennese twelve-note composers, and for four days there was no question of conversations. Except for an afternoon spent in Tours, when Poulenc —the discriminating epicure—purchased the best traditional minced pork of Touraine, the finest fruits, the tenderest meat, the freshest fish and the tastiest cheese (he was very fond of cheese) he occupied himself entirely with correcting his proofs.

"There is a time to every purpose", he must have thought, echoing the Bible.

Indeed, the very next day he said to me: "That's it! The proofs are all corrected. I'll make them up into a handsome parcel which perhaps you'll be kind enough to take to the post. I'm not going out, it's too cold. You can send it express by registered post to Madame Salabert, my publisher. That way I'll be sure she gets it tomorrow morning."

Once the parcel was tied up he said to me, with a kind of seriousness that impressed me at the time and overcomes me today: "This will be my last religious work."

On my return from the village he talked to me about our

Preface

conversations, helped me sketch out a plan of the one about the twelve-note composers, and gave me the necessary material: books, photographs, references for dates, etc., so that that very evening, after the traditional music session, during which he played to me Webern's *Six Pieces for Orchestra*, I only had to write the first draft of my interview.

Next morning I had scarcely finished washing when Francis came into my room. I saw by his look that this wasn't one of his good days.

"If only you knew how my music gets on my nerves," he said, slumping down into an armchair. "I can't listen to it any longer. *Les Carmélites* especially bores me stiff. Everything I write oozes tedium."

As I was protesting he insisted: "I know what I'm saying. It's all foreign to me, it's all dead."

I retorted that since *Les Carmélites* was bound up with a painful period in his life, it was only natural that the opera should seem unbearable to him.

"Not a bit of it," he replied, "there's no connection at all. I never associate a work with events."

"You won't convince anyone by claiming that your music is boring..."

"Yes. *Les Carmélites* is a bore. I'd swop the whole score for *La Voix humaine*."

"That's your opinion," I said. "Anyway, there's something you can be sure of. Even if I hear only three or four bars by chance on the radio, I can say without ever being mistaken: 'That's by Poulenc!'"

"Pooh! pooh! pooh!" he said, with the pout of a spoilt child.

He got up, went towards the window, and, looking at the gloomy winter landscape, he groaned: "I don't like the country! At heart I'm like my sister, I only like Paris. We're genuine Paris people."

My Friends and Myself

He sighed deeply, shook his head as if to dispel that sense of doubt with which all creative artists are well acquainted, and then went back to his work-room. A few moments later, the opening choruses of Prokofiev's opera *War and Peace* could be heard drifting up.

When I went to see him again he let me hear his *Élégie pour cor*, his *Sonate pour flûte*, and then the one for oboe. Referring to the clarinet sonata, which he had recently finished, he told me: "I shall write another for bassoon. And then I'll have covered the whole range of wind instruments."

At that moment the telephone rang. It was in the hall and I could hear Francis' exclamations from a distance. He was saying: "No! Upon my word! It's not possible! You don't say! Oh no! It's too much . . ." I noted once again how, as he grew older, his way of registering surprise resembled his uncle's, Marcel Royer, whom he had loved so much. I commented on it to him as soon as he was back in the room; he agreed that it had often been said to him and told me that his sister had just reported the death of one of their elderly female cousins. She died suddenly on a platform in the Métro.

"What a lovely death!" he cried. "That's how I'd want to go, instantly, without suffering."

As he had made the same remark at the time of Jacques Thibaud's tragic death, I suddenly felt seized by anxiety, without, however, any logical reason. But the fact of loving a human being deeply implies that one gives way on occasion to inexplicable anxieties; and besides, for some time now I'd glimpsed in Francis a weariness, not of the mind but organic, which preyed on me. That was what made me say to him one day: "Don't decide to die before I do, I'd be too sad."

He said nothing in reply, but granted me a smile in which all his basic kindliness appeared.

Without fearing death Poulenc dreaded its warnings; he could not bear the idea that a stroke might paralyse him.

Preface

Thank God he was spared it. Carried off by a heart attack, he had exactly the death he had hoped for.

I wouldn't like to say that he thought about it. Nevertheless, the day he heard of his cousin's death he drew my attention to a charming little pastel portrait of Marie-Blanche de Polignac by Vuillard: "Dear Marie-Blanche," he murmured in affected tones. "When she realized that the end was certain, she walked around her apartments on the arm of her companion pointing out one after another the items she wanted to leave to her friends. 'This portrait will be for Poulenc, don't forget,' she said. That's how I came to inherit it." He thought for a moment, then, turning towards me, he said with marked seriousness: "That's how it should be done."

Now that he is no longer alive I can remember everything at Noizay which should have put me on the alert. We are constantly given signs which our warm-bloodedness and appetite for life prevent us from recognizing. We only realize them when the inevitable has happened.

However, the end of our visit was in sight. The evening before our return to Paris Francis lit a great wood-fire on the hearth, settled himself comfortably into his chair, and gave himself up to the pleasure of conversation. He was dazzling. Once again I admired the range of his culture. His knowledge of music, painting and literature was bewildering. Evoking the memories of his youth he brought to life again, with spirit, buffoonery and a fantastic sense of observation, the surrealists, the Princesse de Polignac, Diaghilev, Wanda Landowska, Anna de Noailles, not forgetting Satie, Georges Auric, Cocteau, Éluard, and Marcel Proust, from whose *Sodome et Gomorrhe* he read a passage about Monsieur de Charlus . . . There were so many more. I questioned him about the "pilgrimage" he went on to Mödling, near Vienna, where Arnold Schoenberg lived.

"You went there in 1922, to be precise, with the singer

My Friends and Myself

Marya Freund and Darius Milhaud. Was it curiosity about the composer rather than fellow-feeling that led you to Schoenberg?" I asked.

"It was curiosity. Schoenberg had fascinated me for a long time. In 1914 I was fifteen years old, I'd bought Webern's *Six Pieces* (opus 19), dating from 1911, and I'd been attracted by the novelty of music that didn't resemble Stravinsky's. I was busy weighing up the great importance of this musical purification. Webern, Berg and Schoenberg constituted the open sesame of a new musical technique. Very interested, by 1914, in the curious vocal conception of *Pierrot Lunaire*, I had to wait for the performance by Marya Freund and Milhaud at the Weiner Concerts before I understood the range of the work. In May, 1920, in the first issue of the Jean Cocteau group's little paper, *Le Coq*, Paul Morand wrote the following message: 'Arnold Schoenberg, the "Six" composers take off their hats to you.' Of course, there was never any question of my subjecting myself to the Schoenbergian doctrines, but as I was curious about whatever music was farthest removed from me, I gladly accepted the suggestion, put to me by Marya Freund and Milhaud, of a trip to Vienna. Once there, Gustav Mahler's widow received us every day; it was in her house that I got to know Schoenberg, Berg and Webern. I was present there at a double performance of *Pierrot Lunaire*, the first with the wonderful pianist Edward Stauermann and the singer Erika Wagner, the second with Marya Freund, conducted by Milhaud."

"Was there any great difference between the performances?"

"A very clear difference. The Freund-Milhaud performance was more sensual than Erika Wagner's. She had a preciseness I was to meet with again afterwards in the recording of Pierre Boulez' *Picarsic*."

Then I asked him if he could picture Schoenberg for me.

"Very easily," he said. "He looked like a little professor

Preface

from some German Conservatoire. I lunched with him at Mödling. He lived there with his first wife, who was very unaffected, in a charming house with a garden. On the walls were pictures he'd painted, very obviously inspired by Kokoschka. And just think, the moment we sat down to table in the drawing-room with its open window—the weather was superb—a little boy who was playing in the garden threw his ball so awkwardly, or skilfully—you never know with children—that it fell right in the middle of the soup tureen. The soup spurted up like a geyser, flooding the tablecloth and ... the guests."

He brightened up at this memory, but since I wanted to know more about it I asked him to tell me whether, in 1922, he foresaw the immense international influence of the Viennese school. He thought for a moment and said: "On one hand Stravinsky's sun was so warm and, on the other, Hindemith's neo-classicism so tempting to musicians eager for a certain type of formalism, that the subtle innovations of the Viennese didn't find the climate in which they could flourish. But then came the 1939-1945 war. It is the business of wars to make obsolete what has been done before them. The young composers found in the Viennese school the fermentation, the yeast they needed to make their musical pies rise."

I then hinted, not without malice, I admit: "So that if you were twenty years old now you'd submit yourself without hesitation to serial and twelve-note disciplines?"

I must be truthful and confess that he said nothing in reply and that he turned the conversation to Bartók, whose work became known to him during his stay in Vienna. Poulenc did not meet him there—Bartók was then in Budapest—but when Bartók came to Paris in 1922 for the first performance of his second piano concerto, to be conducted by Pierre Monteux, Poulenc invited him home to dinner with ... Erik Satie.

"What an idea!" I said. "To bring together two composers

so diametrically opposed. What happened? The sparks must have flown."

"Not at all. They looked at each other as a Martian would look at an inhabitant of the moon."

I remarked to him that Bartók's influence seemed to me less important than that of the Viennese.

"It's obvious," he agreed. "Bartók didn't bring the same potential for novelty. It's natural that young composers should derive from Webern, while at the present moment there is no reason why they should derive from Bartók or Stravinsky."

Talking afterwards about his plans, he confided that he wanted to find a libretto for an opera, an opéra-comique or even an operetta, provided it was of high literary quality. He mentioned the name of René Clair, although he had not yet been in touch with him. There is no doubt about it: such a collaboration would have given us an exquisite work, essentially French and Parisian into the bargain.

I thought about it in the train taking me back to Paris through chilly weather that was turning harsher and harsher. Francis had caught a cold and complained bitterly about it. He looked forward without pleasure to the concerts he was to give in Holland with Denise Duval. I only expected to see him again on the date arranged for our recordings, the 30th January. It didn't happen like that at all. His sense of friendship wouldn't allow of it. I dined twice with him, the first time before a performance at the Comédie Française, the second before spending an evening at the Théâtre de l'Ambigu.

We arrived there "before the candles were lit". We were alone in the orchestra stalls. And Francis went into raptures: "What a lovely theatre! Look at the charming red of the drop-curtain! and all those mirrors round the auditorium! Those delicate little balconies! Look at the amphitheatre, too. It reminds me of those Daumier lithographs, you know, where

Preface

the faces of the spectators leaning towards the stage are lit from below. It's marvellous!"

The play delighted him so much that he wanted to go and congratulate the actors. The dusty wings at the Ambigu and the comfortless dressing-rooms delighted him quite as much.

"How I love that old theatre," he told me as we walked towards the Métro station. "You feel they've always acted plays there. It's soaked in the atmosphere."

And when we were sitting in our carriage: "You get out at Vavins, of course. It's right beside your door. I'll get out at Saint-Michel."

I was surprised. "Why Saint-Michel? Odéon is much nearer your home."

He gave a start. "Oh no, my word! Definitely not at Odéon!"

I smiled. Once again he had betrayed his never-ending quest for cheerfulness. One must admit that walking up the dark rue de l'Odéon has nothing very lively about it, whereas the boulevard Saint-Michel, its illuminated shop windows, its cafés and pavements filled with students cutting their lectures, offers enough to entertain the gloomiest soul.

When we arrived at his station Francis shook hands and said: "I'll see you next Wednesday, the 30th, at half-past six at the recording studio in the rue François 1er. Au revoir."

He made his way to the exit in that lazy way peculiar to him, the feet lightly turned outwards, the felt hat set back on his head like a halo, the roomy Raglan overcoat swaying to the rhythm of his step.

My eyes did not leave him until the crowd of travellers around him and the angle of a corridor hid him from sight . . .

The next time I saw him was on his deathbed.

Now that he is no more, now that the immeasurable distance that separates the living from the dead widens day by day, it comforts me to think that his work perpetuates him. It is in

My Friends and Myself

his music that future generations will discover him as he really was: in love with life, mischievous, good-hearted, tender and pert, sad and serenely mystical, at once monk and playboy. The conversations you are about to read show him in all his completeness. We have refrained from correcting them in any way at all because we were so keen to preserve their spontaneity. We have even gone so far as to respect the emphasis with which Poulenc underlined certain words. The reader will thus have the feeling that he is hearing Poulenc speak. I hope, too, that the reader will appreciate Poulenc's enthusiasm for his masters, the companions of his youth and his friends. If music has lost a great composer, his intimates and all those who had the happiness of knowing him closely lament the death of a friend who was not only incomparable but irreplaceable.

Stéphane Audel.

April, 1963.

I
My Youth

I

PARIS and NOGENT-sur-MARNE

Stéphane Audel. Francis, I'd like our conversations to show Poulenc as he really is. With this idea in mind I shall follow a strictly chronological order, which leads me naturally to ask you where you were born and to talk to me about your earliest family memories.

Francis Poulenc. I was born in Paris . . . in the very heart of Paris, a few yards away from the Church of the Madeleine, on the 7th January, 1899. My father came originally from Aveyron. He was, together with my two uncles, at the head of a very old chemical products firm which eventually became Rhône-Poulenc. My mother, of purely Parisian descent (since the beginning of the nineteenth century her family had only intermarried with Parisians), came from a line of cabinet-makers, bronze workers and tapestry weavers.

S.A. Did your parents like music?

F.P. Yes, my parents were very musical and everyone loved music in the two families. However, even if my father rarely missed a rehearsal at the Colonne concerts, or a first night at the Opéra or the Opéra-Comique, he did not play an instrument; whereas my mother was an excellent pianist. At that time young ladies of middle-class family did not develop their technique as far as they do today, when everyone wonders if they have found a practical outlet for their talents. This didn't prevent my mother playing Mozart, Schumann and Chopin

My Friends and Myself

delightfully. Besides, she'd studied the piano with Madam Riss-Arbeau, one of Liszt's last pupils. My mother had a charming touch and perfect musical understanding allied to great virtuosity. She idolized Mozart, Schubert and Chopin. My father preferred Beethoven, Berlioz, César Franck and Massenet! I must say that I shared my mother's taste while still a small child, and that I put Mozart highest of all in music.

S.A. Tell us about your uncle Marcel Royer, the doyen of subscription-ticket holders at the Odéon theatre, where I knew him. All his friends called him Papoum. How did he acquire this odd nickname?

F.P. It came about because, as a child, I couldn't pronounce *parrain* [godfather], and I said Papoum. Papoum was the very model of the old cultured Parisian. He used to paint only for his own pleasure, under the influence of Toulouse-Lautrec—alas!

S.A. Marcel Royer lived in that cheerful building where you live now. All the windows open out on the greenery of the Jardin du Luxembourg. His flat, filled with Japanese curios, lacquer-work and bronzes, associated itself in my mind with the "artistic" style made famous by the Goncourt brothers.

F.P. You're right. It was exactly in the Goncourt style that people poke gentle fun at these days. In my uncle's flat a pair of very valuable porcelain vases stood next to a charming Japanese knick-nack worth about twopence.

S.A. I think you saw Papoum often when you were a little boy?

F.P. Certainly. He was always coming to see my mother, and through him—how exciting it was!—I heard talk of theatres, pictures, concerts, while I was thought to be busy working my toy railway under the table.

Paris and Nogent-sur-Marne

S.A. Where did you spend the summer months at that time?

F.P. At Nogent-sur-Marne, with my maternal grandmother. As I've often told you, Stéphane, the Royers (that was my mother's maiden name), were such confirmed city-dwellers that ten miles out of Paris seemed distant country to them. Nogent, on the other hand, was my grandfather's home town. One of our ancestors was a market gardener there at the time of Louis-Philippe in the eighteen-thirties.

S.A. One can't deny that the twin influence of Paris and Nogent permeates your music. Nogent-sur-Marne often reappears and gives your work (I'm talking especially about your paradoxical piano concerto) a flavour I won't call common —which is more than I mean to say—but popular, rather like "street music" . . .

F.P. I've often been reproached about my "street music" side. Its genuineness has been suspected, and yet there's nothing more genuine in me. Our two families ran their business houses in the Marais district, full of lovely old houses, a few yards from the Bastille. From childhood onwards I've associated café tunes with the Couperin Suites in a common love without distinguishing between them.

S.A. At present you often withdraw to your house at Noizay, near Amboise. Since a very great part of your music was written there, many of your admirers think you're a native of Touraine.

F.P. "Poulenc, the man from Touraine" is a label I've not succeeded in getting rid of. Believe me, there's nothing of Touraine about me, near or far. I chose Touraine because it is pretty country and neutral enough for me to work freely.

S.A. Do you think the calm atmosphere and those peacefully arranged landscapes of the Loire have been able to influence your work?

My Friends and Myself

F.P. Not in the slightest. My twin heredity, Paris and Aveyron, has nothing at all to do with that rigorously formal-looking countryside, so rich in writers, so poor in musicians. Touraine has never produced, alas!, a musical Ronsard or Balzac.

S.A. I think, rather, it was your dearly-loved Aunt Liénard who gave you the taste for Touraine.

F.P. Actually, it was because of my Aunt Liénard that I settled in Touraine. She owned a charming house near Amboise where she spent four months a year and lived the rest of the time in Cannes. Her stepfather, a native of Touraine born and bred, was the ornamental sculptor spoken of by Balzac—his friend—in *La Cousine Bette*. What an astonishing woman my Aunt Liénard was! She loved music, (she'd heard Wagner conduct *Lohengrin* at Brussels and been present at one of Liszt's last concerts in Italy), and a few days before the first performance of Stravinsky's *Noces* in Paris she wrote to me: "I'm definitely bringing forward my departure from the south by a fortnight because I want to hear your beloved Stravinsky's new work." She was then seventy-eight years old!

S.A. Let's come back to your early childhood. I have a photograph showing you at the age of three, wearing a little dress and a round straw hat with a ribbon, in front of a tiny piano. "My first concert," you wrote on it. This seems to prove that you genuinely felt the call of your vocation very early.

F.P. At the age of two I was, in fact, given a charming little piano, white lacquered with cherries painted on it. Dear little piano, how I loved it! When I was eight it was still kept in the toy cupboard, but when I reached the age of nine I stupidly thought it unworthy of me and it was given away. At two years old I sight-read everything I thought was music

Paris and Nogent-sur-Marne

—that is, department-store catalogues and old railway timetables—at that little piano.

S.A. Could you tell me when for the first time you felt you were intended for music?

F.P. As far back as I can go in memory my sole preoccupation was music. That excellent tenor Edmont Clément, a close friend of my uncle Royer, was always coming to our house. When I was ten I heard him sing *Manon* at the Opéra Comique. What a des Grieux he was! I was fascinated, and until the age of fifteen I dreamed of becoming a singer. In the end I had to be satisfied with what I've become, because when my voice broke I was left with the composer's typical sorry squawk.

S.A. I would imagine, Francis, that in your youth you wrote a work symbolizing your love of Nogent-sur-Marne?

F.P. No, in youth I was much more pretentious. At the age of fifteen—in 1914—I wrote a *Processional for the Cremation of a Mandarin*—that alone would be enough to . . . obviously inspired by Stravinsky's *Le Rossignol*. It was only last year that I dared write a café waltz for two pianos that conjures up the Nogent of my childhood.

S.A. What's it called?

F.P. *L'Embarquement pour Cythère*, of course, because its aim is to evoke the Isle of Love and the Isle of Beauty, with their Nogent taverns and gardens and their sentimental, tongue-in-cheek accordions.

2

STUDIES: KOECHLIN and VIÑES

Stéphane Audel. From our first conversation it emerged that your vocation showed itself at an early age. How old were you when you began to study music seriously?

Francis Poulenc. Because of a delicate childhood, the traditional education my father put me through, and finally my anticipated departure in 1918 for the Front, my musical education went in fits and starts. When I was five my mother put my fingers on the keyboard, and she soon took as her assistant a lady whose name I forget but who impressed me more with her vast bespangled hats and grey dresses than with her mediocre teaching. At the age of eight I was extremely fortunate to be entrusted daily to a lady who was private coach to Mademoiselle Boutet de Monvel, César Franck's niece, and she had very good technical principles. Every evening I worked hard with her for an hour on my return from school, and when I had a few free minutes during the day I would run to my piano and sight-read. My lack of technique didn't prevent me getting by reasonably well, and so it was that in 1913—I was fourteen—I was able to enjoy Schoenberg's *Six Little Pieces*, Bartók's wild *Allegro*, and all of Stravinsky, Debussy and Ravel.

S.A. Why is it that you didn't go through the usual grades of the Conservatoire?

F.P. You've touched on a sensitive spot there, Stéphane. My

Studies: Koechlin and Viñes

mother, who felt immediately that music was my only vocation, would certainly have let me enter the Conservatoire. Artists had always been accepted in her family, and it seemed to her quite natural. But my father, despite his love for music, was unable to agree that an industrialist's son shouldn't sit for his two school-leaving exams. "He can do what he likes afterwards," my father used to repeat. The result was that, continually sacrificing my conventional education to my beloved piano, I was a less than indifferent pupil at school. I only just passed my first exam, thanks to a brilliant essay on Diderot which made up for some woeful science marks. During that period Monsieur Muccioli, an Italian 'cello teacher at Nogent-sur-Marne, improved my knowledge of theory and an organist friend put me through my paces in harmony. Then, when I was eighteen, after finishing my exams, I went into the army. So it was only three years afterwards, in 1921, that I began to study composition seriously.

S.A. With whom?

F.P. As it was really too late after doing my army service to enter the Conservatoire, Darius Milhaud advised me to apply to Charles Koechlin, who supervised my studies in counterpoint.

S.A. Would you, please, say what Charles Koechlin was like as a teacher?

F.P. After the death of André Gédalge, Charles Koechlin was by far the best teacher of counterpoint in France. His knowledge was fantastic, but the most wonderful thing about him was the way he adapted to the pupil. Having felt, as a result, that like most Latins I was more of a harmonist than a contrapuntist, he made me write four-part realizations of Bach chorale themes as well as the usual counterpoint exercises. This work fascinated me and had a decisive influence on me. It was thanks to this that I acquired a feeling for choral music.

My Friends and Myself

S.A. I think a large number of other composers of your generation owe a lot to Koechlin.

F.P. Yes, there are many of us who owe a debt of gratitude to Charles Koechlin. Henri Sauguet studied with him too, and so did quite a few others who forget to say so.

S.A. How did you work at the time? Was the method you followed then the same as the one you use today?

F.P. I work more at my desk now than in the early days, but I've always used the piano a lot. When I was twenty I felt rather ashamed about it and envied Milhaud his ability to compose in railway carriages; until the day when Stravinsky told me of his famous conversation with Rimsky-Korsakov. Stravinsky was indulging in a bit of self-pity about writing too much at the piano and Rimsky replied: "Some write without the piano, others with it. You belong to the second category, that's all."

S.A. Let's come back to your piano studies. Who did you work with besides your first anonymous teachers?

F.P. At the age of fifteen, as I've already told you, I got by reasonably well, no more. On the advice of a family friend, Madame Sienkiewicz, I was taken to Ricardo Viñes whom I admired enormously. For at that time, in 1914, he was the only virtuoso to play Debussy and Ravel. That meeting with Viñes was a turning point in my life: I owe him everything. If Koechlin enabled me eventually to perfect my craft, it's really to Viñes that I owe my first flights in music and everything I know about the piano.

S.A. Tell us something about him as a pianist. Don't neglect the teacher, either, since he was the man who enabled you to become what you are: a pianist with a uniquely personal talent.

F.P. Dear Viñes! I could talk to you about him for hours,

Studies: Koechlin and Viñes

I loved him so much and was so proud of his affection for me. He was a most delightful man, a bizarre hidalgo with enormous moustachios, a flat-brimmed sombrero in the purest Spanish style, and button boots which he used to rap my shins with when I didn't change the pedalling enough. No one better than Viñes could handle pedalling, that essential factor in modern music. He succeeded in playing crisply even through a wash of pedalling! And what cunning he showed in distinguishing between *staccato* and full *legato*! The great pianist Marcelle Meyer, who was his most brilliant pupil, told me one day after finishing a performance of *Petrouchka*: "It wasn't as difficult as all that, thanks to Viñes!"

S.A. Viñes certainly deserves a place in the history of contemporary music. He was a *descubridor*: a discoverer. As you've just said, he revealed Debussy, Ravel, Satie, Mompou, and so many others to music lovers! Don't you think, Francis, that Viñes' career wasn't what it might have been, simply because of his independence and because his total lack of academicism kept the general public away from him? Léon-Paul Fargue, who knew him well, wrote: "There were three words that seemed for ever shut out from his heart and his vocabulary, three sordid words that did not have even the slightest meaning for him: intrigue, careerism, compromise." "Discoverers" such as he was exist in all the arts. Others less qualified then benefit from their revelations and cast the initiator into oblivion. Isn't that a case of glaring injustice?

F.P. Yes, people have been unjust to Viñes. Since he wasn't a Romantic, his right to be called a virtuoso was questioned; but believe me, technically he'd have been able to teach a thing or two to many of those pillars of the concert platform who line up Chopin after Chopin at the starting-gate.

S.A. The combined teaching of Koechlin and Viñes brought

about the birth of your earliest works, since it was then that you decided to compose, wasn't it?

F.P. I'd already been composing before getting to know Viñes and even quite a long time before studying with Koechlin, since my *Bestiaire* songs date from 1918, and I didn't work with Koechlin until 1921. But each of these teachers deeply influenced the direction I took at different times. Moreover, it was Viñes who gave the first performance of all my early piano works. The oldest of my published pieces is a *Pastorale* dedicated to Viñes. I wrote it one year before the *Mouvements perpétuels*, in 1917, that is. It was part of a suite of three pastoral pieces. In 1929, after Alfredo Casella had asked why I'd put them on the shelf, I re-wrote the first and added a *Toccata*—very well known now, thanks to Horowitz' fantastic playing—and an *Hymne*—a close relation of my *Concert champêtre*—which is too rarely played these days.

3

LES SIX and DIAGHILEV

Stéphane Audel. If you're willing, let's start on your emergence as a composer. In what year did you make your first contact with the concert-going public?

Francis Poulenc. This occurred with my *Rapsodie nègre* for chamber orchestra at the Théâtre du Vieux Colombier in December, 1917.

S.A. At the very moment when your friendship with Erik Satie began?

F.P. No, my meeting with Satie dates from several months before. In April, 1917, Diaghilev let off yet another bomb with his Russian Ballet by putting on Erik Satie's ballet *Parade*, with scenery by Picasso. I was conquered! With all the injustice of youth, and although I idolized Debussy, I agreed to disown him a little because I was so eager for the new inspiration Satie and Picasso were bringing us. That was the time when Ricardo Viñes introduced me to Satie. He'd heard tell of me from Georges Auric whom I'd met several months previously at Viñes' house and who'd then become what he has never since ceased to be for me: my true brother in spirit. Satie was suspicious of the young Poulenc because he came of middle-class stock, but my admiration for *Parade* seemed so genuine to him that he adopted me completely. An amusing circumstance brought us still closer together a few weeks later. Not expecting to leave so early for the Front, I wanted to study composition seriously. Viñes sent me to Paul Dukas who gave me a very pleasant reception and examined my first attempts with indulgence; but Dukas, since he gave few lessons during the war, thought it better to pass me on to Paul Vidal, the composer of *La Korrigane,* a Breton ballet that used to be well known. He was a tall man with a ruddy complexion. Scarcely had I shown him my *Rapsodie nègre* than he flew into a frightful rage, told me I was playing practical jokes and threatened a portion of my anatomy with his foot if I didn't leave his office "im-med-iate-ly!" Next day, told of the incident by Auric, Satie sent me the following note:

Cher ami,
 I'd like to see you. You seem lost to me but easy to find again. Suggest a date.
 Who can be giving you such strange advice? It's funny. Never mix your schools: the result is an explosion, which after all is quite natural. What's more, if I'm to give you useful advice, I shall have to know what you plan to do and what you can do. Your application to Vidal was that of an amateur pupil, not an artist pupil. He showed you that himself. He's an old dyed-in-the-wool prima donna who's put you off your stroke. Laugh it off, old chap.
Yours ever,
ERIK SATIE[1]

Our close friendship dates from that letter.

S.A. Was that the time when you knew Jane Bathori?

F.P. My dear Stéphane, probably thinking I'd talked too much you took the words out of my mouth at the very moment when I was about to say that it was thanks to Jane Bathori that my *Rapsodie nègre* was put on at the concerts

---

[1] The paragraphing of this letter is different from that used in the version given in: *Francis Poulenc, Correspondence, 1915–1963,* collected by Hélène de Wendel, Editions du Seuil, 1967. [Translator.]

Les Six and Diaghilev

in the Théâtre du Vieux Colombier. Jacques Copeau, who was then in America with Louis Jouvet and Charles Dullin, had authorized Bathori to manage the Vieux Colombier exactly as she thought fit. She gave a series of productions there, including the first performance of Honegger's *Dits des jeux du monde* and several concerts at which Tailleferre, Auric, Durey, Honegger, Milhaud and I played the music. This, although it wasn't done deliberately—and I'd like to emphasize the point that it wasn't deliberate—marked the beginning of the group that became known as *les Six*. What didn't we owe to dear Bathori! The first to sing Debussy, Ravel, Roussel, she has never stopped prospecting for new music. Today, on the French radio, she is still looking for new songs, songs in which she accompanies her pupils with so much art.

S.A. It would be interesting to know what sort of reception the Vieux Colombier audiences gave to these new works and what their reactions were. Have you any recollections about this?

F.P. I vividly remember the moment when young Arthur Honegger, dressed as a troubadour, played the drum for the play of *Robin et Marion*. As far as my *Rapsodie nègre* is concerned, the performance didn't pass without incident. This work, a reflection of the taste for negro art which had flourished since 1912 under the impetus of Apollinaire, included four instrumental movements and a vocal interlude. The latter was a setting of an imitation negro poem by a friend who signed himself "Makoko Kangourou". You can just imagine the effect *that* had! At the last minute the singer threw in the sponge, saying it was too silly and that he didn't want to look a fool. Quite unexpectedly, masked by a big music stand, I had to sing that interlude myself. Since I was already in uniform, you can just imagine the unusual effect produced by a soldier bawling out songs in pseudo-Malagasy!

My Friends and Myself

S.A. Let's turn to more serious things again.

F.P. Alas!

S.A. I'd like to get round to discussing the make-up of Les Six.

F.P. As you know, Les Six consisted of Germaine Tailleferre, Georges Auric, Louis Durey, Honegger, Milhaud and me. Already, at the Vieux Colombier concerts, our names used to turn up again often on the same programme. In a Montparnasse studio, under the title "Lyre et Palette", we'd become associated with the artists Picasso, Braque, Modigliani and Juan Gris, who exhibited there. Ricardo Viñes played my Mouvements perpétuels for the first time in that studio. Our names only had to be linked together as a team several times for a critic needing a slogan to baptize the French Les Six, on the model of the famous "Five" Russian composers. We had never had any common aesthetic and our musical styles have always been dissimilar. Our likes and dislikes were opposed. Thus, Honegger has never liked Satie's music, and Schmitt, whom he then admired, was a pet aversion for Milhaud and me.

S.A. If my memory's correct, Darius Milhaud was just back from Brazil, where Paul Claudel, the French Ambassador, had taken him. Wasn't it on his return from the tropics that Milhaud joined up with you? You'd already taken him under your wing.

F.P. Yes, Milhaud's actual presence among us dates from his return from Brazil. He instantly became for me an incomparable friend whom I deeply admire. What a bracing source of music he is, and what a magnificent character!

S.A. And Jean Cocteau, whose name keeps cropping up in all the avant-garde movements of the time? Did he play a part in Les Six?

Les Six and Diaghilev

F.P. Jean Cocteau is always attracted by novelty of every sort. He wasn't our theorist, but our friend and our brilliant spokesman. To tell the truth, his little musical summary, *Le Coq et l'Arlequin*, is a disguised defence of Satie's aesthetic against Stravinsky's. It is impossible to regard it as a manifesto of *Les Six* because Arthur Honegger's violent and romantic art is alone enough to contradict it.

S.A. Cocteau's name is linked, for the present generation at least, with the history of the Russian Ballet. Its brilliant director Serge Diaghilev acted like a magnet on poets, painters, musicians. It was an honour for you, Francis, that he recognized your talent and decided to produce your first ballet, *Les Biches*. Will you say something about Diaghilev?

F.P. Diaghilev, the irreplaceable Diaghilev, was a sorcerer, a magician. No sooner had he achieved success than he would burn what he had once worshipped (in appearance at least) so as to keep pressing ahead. So it was that from 1917 onwards, smitten by everything to do with modern art, he paired off painter and musician with rare felicity. That's why he commissioned me to do a ballet with Marie Laurencin, at the same time as he asked Auric and Braque for one. That's how *Les Biches* was born.

S.A. What year was *Les Biches* put on?

F.P. The first performance was at Monte Carlo on the 6th January, 1924.

S.A. Who provided the plot of the ballet?

F.P. Strictly speaking there was no plot to *Les Biches*. Diaghilev's idea was to produce a sort of *Les Sylphides* up-to-date, in other words a ballet of atmosphere. Then I got the idea of placing modern *fêtes galantes* in a large, all-white country drawing-room with a huge sofa in Laurencin blue as the only piece of furniture. Twenty charming and flirtatious women frolicked about there with three handsome, strapping young fellows dressed as oarsmen. There was nothing to be seen of these lovers' sports, nor were you able even to imagine "the worst". In this lay all the allusive art of Nijinska, the choreographer. She was, as you probably know, the great Nijinsky's sister. For the first performance in Paris, André Messager, that master of French operetta and unrivalled conductor of *Pelléas et Mélisande,* did me the honour of conducting my work. During the ballet the light on his music desk went out, but in spite of everything he brought my score safely home to port. (It was my first venture in orchestration.) Anyway, I completely re-scored *Les Biches* in 1940. As for the dancers, it was in *Les Biches* that Nemtchinova made her unforgettable début. She was unknown up to then, but Diaghilev had sensed that she was the girl for the part. He never hesitated to reveal unknowns like that when he considered them to be unique. That's why he was Providence itself for musicians, artists and dancers.

4

LANDOWSKA, BERNAC, ÉLUARD
and some SONGS

Stéphane Audel. Apart from your meeting with Ricardo Viñes and Jane Bathori, what have been the other decisive encounters in your career?

Francis Poulenc. The three great decisive encounters in my career, the ones that have deeply influenced my art, have been with Wanda Landowska, Pierre Bernac and Paul Éluard. To each in their different spheres I want to pay the tribute of my gratitude here.

S.A. You've just mentioned Wanda Landowska's name. Talk about her first as a woman.

F.P. Wanda Landowska is one of those rare women who give me the impression of genius in its purest state. By that I mean that like Colette she is gloriously feminine and draws all her strength from that femininity. Patience, determination, discernment are the true qualities of the bee. So they are of Wanda Landowska. I came across her in America last year, seventy-three years old, rich with splendid health and tremendous experience, as vital as when I'd known her thirty years ago and as she has always remained ever since. As you know, the first performance of Manuel de Falla's *El retablo de Maeso Pedro* took place at the home of the Princesse de Polignac, a great friend of the arts and of artists. Falla conducted rehearsals and Wanda was at the harpsichord. It's worth mentioning that this was the first time the harpsichord was accepted in modern music. Ricardo Viñes, dear old Viñes again, who was operating the puppets with his nephew and the painter Ortiz, introduced me to Landowska. Immediately she invited me to her home, and, since then, I've always been a favourite of hers. Nothing makes me prouder than this friendship. I'm always among the first to receive one of those gramophone records, dedicated and beribboned, in which she hands on to the public the great classic tradition.

S.A. Did you write your *Concert champêtre* for her?

F.P. Of course, it was for her. After Falla's harpsichord concerts, when I was lucky enough to follow all the rehearsals, Wanda asked me to write her a concerto. I got the idea of composing a *concert champêtre* with something of the atmosphere of the Forêt de Saint-Leu where Rosseau and Diderot used to go for walks, the place where Couperin, like Landowska, had stayed. A sharp-tongued critic thought to upset me by writing: "In the last movement of this *Concert champêtre* we suddenly hear, Heaven knows why, the echoes of barrack trumpet calls. A pretty sort of countryside!"[1] He was absolutely right! For a townsman like me it *was* a pretty sort of countryside, that Parisian suburb where so many eighteenth-century houses drowse on among the market gardens that supply the Halles in Paris. At Saint-Leu-la-Forêt Landowska had created a real paradise that war and nazi anti-semitism have spoiled so disgustingly. Alas! she will never go back there, but, like all strong personalities, she takes her home with her everywhere she travels. In Connecticut, at Lakeville, you find yourself in Saint-Leu again, just as at Stravinsky's in

---

[1] This was Gabriel Marcel (b. 1889), better known as philosopher and dramatist. He has himself set many French poems to music with the aid of his wife, who notates them for him. He is very proud of his little effusions. [Translator.]

Landowska, Bernac, Éluard and some songs

Hollywood it's the same atmosphere as in his homes at Biarritz and Nice.

S.A. Has Wanda Landowska's matchless technique influenced yours at the piano?

F.P. No, because the harpsichord is as different from the piano as the organ, but thanks to her I've been able to grasp Bach's harpsichord works in their full beauty—a beauty that the piano only distorts.

S.A. Tell us now about your favourite singer, Pierre Bernac. A collaboration that's lasted for eighteen years implies a total fellow-feeling in art. You've always gone everywhere together, and it would be interesting to know how the idea of collaboration came to you.

F.P. Pierre Bernac had already given the first performance of my *Chansons gaillardes* in 1927, but we'd completely lost sight of each other until 1934, when *Figaro* sent me to Salzburg as music correspondent. Bernac was working there at the time with the great German singer Warlich. An American lady had decided to give a private Debussy concert in her home. Lifar had already danced *L'Après-midi d'un faune* and a very young conductor at the beginning of his career, Herbert von Karajan, had conducted a long Debussy programme. It was past midnight when this American lady had some Debussy sung to us out of doors, under a weeping willow in beautiful moonlight, while, for the benefit of people who felt the cold, a Canadian pianist played Debussy preludes inside the house. You can judge the lady's appetite! It was all rather ludicrous. I accompanied Bernac and our unexpected success gave us the idea of continuing our association. From that meeting dates a series of concerts we've given pretty well all over the world and especially in America.

S.A. What do you think about the American public?

F.P. It's a wonderful public, because so many people have

My Friends and Myself

emigrated there that as a result, mixing their own old-established culture with a young, healthy and enthusiastic race, there has emerged an audience as spontaneous as it is well-informed. And then, there's the negro public. Listen to this, Stéphane. A negro who was weighing baggage for the Venezuelan airline to New York saw my name on the list of passengers for Caracas and asked me to sign his autograph book. His favourite composers were Debussy in particular, then Stravinsky and Bartók.

S.A. Yes, it's very significant. Since you've mentioned your recitals with Bernac, let's talk about song. It's always been very popular in France. The names of Gounod, Fauré, Debussy, Chabrier and Ravel come easily to my lips. I pretend to forget Duparc, but that's only so that I can ask your opinion of his songs.

F.P. Duparc's songs are very beautiful. He is the only composer who has been able to transpose Baudelaire musically. Duparc always reminds me of the painter Bazille, who, with just a handful of pictures, occupies a select place in French painting. With twelve songs alone to his credit, Duparc is a great composer.

S.A. Who, in your opinion, is the French composer to have reached perfection in the genre?

F.P. Debussy, without the slightest doubt. He was a wonderful composer and a man of taste and culture into the bargain. He knew how to choose poems of worth, while Fauré, paradoxically enough, wrote some of his loveliest songs to mediocre poetry. *Soir*, for example, set to indifferent verse by Albert Samain. This choice of good poetry enabled Debussy to follow the text even in its closest secrets, its silences, what it left unsaid. And what prosody!

S.A. It's quite obvious that the *Chansons de Bilitis*, set to music by Debussy, has such perfect prosody that you can

Landowska, Bernac, Éluard and some songs

recite the lines by carefully following the rhythm the composer has adopted. I'm only a layman in musical technique but I have a feeling that this is the sign of a total fusion between music and poetry.

F.P. You're right; the characteristic of a successful song is that from then on one can never separate it from the poem. The fact, however, that the music sticks to the text like chewing gum must be very tiresome for the poet . . . but it can't be helped!

S.A. What reasons make a composer choose certain poems to set to music? Is it similarity of feeling, an aesthetic kinship, or does the composer obey an unthinking, instinctive impulse?

F.P. I think that the choice of poem must be as instinctive as love. There should be no marriage of reason, otherwise the result is paltry. I've good cause to know something about this. Towards the end of his life Paul Valéry dedicated a charming poem to me, *Dialogues pour deux flûtes*, which he wanted me to set. I admire Valéry as much as Verlaine, Rimbaud or Mallarmé, but, as far as those poets are concerned, I couldn't find a note of music to set their lines. The result was that my *Dialogues pour deux flûtes* (a duet for soprano and baritone, as it turned out), sinks into the worst sort of dullness.

S.A. Let's leave those unfortunate flutes and come to Paul Éluard and his reed-pipe. When did you know him?

F.P. I knew him in 1917, at the same time as Aragon and Breton. I was immediately drawn towards him, but it was only much later that I began to set his poems. I'd always admired Éluard but I couldn't succeed in finding the musical key that would open up his work. For my first concert with Bernac in 1935 I was looking for words to which I could write songs. A little book Éluard had sent me lay on my piano. I made the attempt, and the result was the *Cinq poèmes* which also made

My Friends and Myself

up the first songs I wrote for Bernac. Then I wrote, still with Éluard, some *a cappella* choruses, and in 1938, a long cycle, *Tel jour, telle nuit*, after which came the war. Éluard, who'd given me the possibility of expressing love in music, then offered me, during the Occupation, the means of singing of my hope in one of his major works, *Figure humaine*. It was a cantata for double *a cappella* chorus set to the poems *Poésie et Vérité*, and ending with the poem *Liberté*. Then I did a little *a cappella* cantata, *Un Soir de neige*, and, just recently, the latest song-cycle I've written: *La Fraîcheur et le feu*. If I insist on this listing, it's in order to prove the importance of my meeting with Éluard, whom I mourn so desperately today.

5

APOLLINAIRE and CHABRIER; POULENC'S SECULAR WORKS

Stéphane Audel. Let's talk now about your work on settings of Guillaume Apollinaire. Did you know the author of *Alcools*?

Francis Poulenc. I didn't know Apollinaire well, because I was very young then; I was just seventeen in 1916 when he came back wounded to Paris. However, I met him several times and I can still hear the very special tone of his voice, half ironic, half sad. It makes you think that all poets have a low, gentle voice, because Apollinaire, like Valéry, like Éluard, didn't make much noise. Yet suddenly a great bellow of laughter would shake his heavy figure and then a cascade not of simple words but of ideas would escape from him with the prodigality of a spendthrift. How much modern art owes to Apollinaire! He was the first poet I set to music. In 1918 a reprint of *Bestiaire* with Raoul Dufy's engravings inspired me to write that little group of songs many people know today. Round about 1930, coming back to the medium of song which I'd abandoned for a long time, I set to music a whole series of poems, most of them taken from that very odd collection, *Il y a*. Less perfect but more pointed than *Alcools*, it was put together after Apollinaire's death, with poems from every period between 1904 and 1917. It's in this little-known volume

My Friends and Myself

that you find the most daring and the most whimsical of Apollinaire's work.

S.A. Do you know any stories about Apollinaire, or is there any personal memory that comes to mind?

F.P. I haven't many personal memories of him, but Marie Laurencin, who as everyone knows was his inspiration for several years, told me lots of anecdotes. Here's one I've chosen in the hope of amusing you. At any rate, it shows the poet's gentle irony to perfection. One Monday afternoon Apollinaire asked Marie Laurencin if she'd go out with him. Marie, who didn't have the slightest wish to, replied: "I can't, I'm going to the Louvre." Now at that time museums were always closed on Mondays. Apollinaire didn't bat an eyelid, but some time after that, when the Louvre came up in conversation, he said, without looking at Marie: "Oh, I go there every Monday!"

S.A. What a delightful remark of Apollinaire; it hits him off perfectly, droll and surly all at once. But let's talk about you again and start on your piano works. I'm thinking of *Aubade*. I know you attach importance to that work in particular. When did you compose it?

F.P. *Aubade* is a work I prize. Written for a private performance in 1929, at the time when there were still patrons, it's a choreographic concerto for piano and eighteen instruments. The ballet has been produced, sometimes successfully and sometimes not, throughout the whole world. The only plot I acknowledge, and it's mine, is the simple story of Diana condemned to chastity. For her, every dawn is a reason for sadness. The ballet was recently put on at the Opéra Comique. The production, with lovely scenery by Brianchon, was modest but the sort of thing I wanted.

S.A. Let's turn now to your Concerto for two pianos that all the American newspapers fall over themselves to praise. Why should it be so appreciated in America particularly?

Apollinaire and Chabrier; Poulenc's secular works

F.P. The reason for the Concerto's success in America is very simple. People are very fond indeed of two-piano music over there, and teams of duettists are as numerous as string quartets in Europe. A recording of the Concerto under Dimitri Mitropoulos with the New York Philharmonic contributed a lot to its popularity. Moreover, it sparkles with effect and sounds well.

S.A. When did you compose it?

F.P. In 1932. It was for the Venice Festival, a commission from the Princesse de Polignac.

S.A. Who introduced it, and which orchestra played at the first performance?

F.P. Jacques Février and myself, with the orchestra of La Scala, Milan, under the direction of Désiré Defauw.

S.A. Would you give the Concerto for two pianos a dominant place among your piano works?

F.P. Yes, not so much on account of its intrinsic musical value as because of its success so far as its orchestration is concerned. It can't be denied, for example, that my Concerto for organ and orchestra (also commissioned by the Princesse de Polignac) has much greater density as music.

S.A. I'm going to take the liberty of asking a question that will perhaps surprise you. I'd like you to tell me whether you count among your works any that are "fated". By "fated" I mean a piece that's played too often, that the public demands ceaselessly and that its composer ends up by detesting. It's a sort of ransom that success imposes. Have you had to pay it?

F.P. Certainly, with that *Pastourelle* of mine that every pianist keeps playing over and over again today. I can no longer listen to it, except when it's played by Horowitz, who gives it a new freshness each time. The *Pastourelle* even feeds the animosity of my old mortal enemy Émile Vuillermoz, who never fails to saddle me with it when he wants to talk about me in a belittling way. Not that all this has the slightest importance. Through pride or indifference I don't care about what critics say, and I'm always ready to have a drink with anyone who's slanged me.

S.A. Which proves that you aren't keen on people affecting your mood, that good-tempered mood which you seem to have inherited from Chabrier.

F.P. Ah! Chabrier, I love him as one loves a father! An indulgent father, always merry, his pockets full of tasty tit-bits. Chabrier's music is a treasure house you can never exhaust; I just-could-not-do-without-it! It consoles me on my darkest days, for you know, my faithful friend, I'm a sad man . . . who likes to laugh, as do all sad men.

S.A. I know, but your escapes into happiness are frequent and draw you to write music full of buffoonery, wit and mischief. I'm thinking of Apollinaire's *Les Mamelles de Tirésias*. The original play was produced for the first time on the 24th June, 1917, at the Conservatoire Renée Maubel, with scenery by Serge Férat and incidental music by Germaine Albert-Birot. It's a farcical piece intended to encourage the French to have children. You turned it into an opéra-comique. I'd like to know the reasons for your choice, how and when you composed it.

F.P. I wrote *Les Mamelles de Tirésias* during the summer of 1944. The venture had tempted me for a long time. Isolated for six months in Touraine by the Allied landings, I was able to escape with its help to Zanzibar, the scene of the action, which became for me, quite naturally, Monte Carlo, where Apollinaire spent his first fifteen years tied to his mother's frivolous petticoats.

S.A. What date was it first performed at the Opéra-Comique?

Apollinaire and Chabrier; Poulenc's secular works

F.P. In June, 1948.

S.A. What sort of reception did it get, and who were your singers? Did the elderly subscribers to the Opéra-Comique accept Apollinaire's proposal and the audacities of your score?

F.P. There was a scandal, of course; the subscription ticket-holders and audiences at the Opéra-Comique were dismayed by Apollinaire's gags, but I was lucky enough to be supported by a charming singer I'd discovered: Denise Duval, who has since become a star and the unrivalled "lead" in Ravel's *L'Heure espagnole*. I've every weakness for *Les Mamelles de Tirésias*; I think I prefer this work to everything else I've written. If you want to get an idea of my complex musical personality, you'll find me completely myself as much in *Les Mamelles* as in my *Stabat Mater*.

6

RELIGIOUS WORKS; method of composing

Stéphane Audel. I don't think you'll contradict me if I say that choral and religious music has enabled you fully to realize yourself.

Francis Poulenc. I think, in fact, that I've put the best and the most genuine part of myself into it. Even in the secular choral works, *Sécheresses*, for example, the cantata for chorus and orchestra, and especially *Figure humaine*, I've always brought to it a texture that's very different from the rest of my work. Forgive my lack of modesty, but I have a feeling that in that sphere I've really produced something new, and I'm not far off thinking that if people are still interested in my music fifty years from now it'll be more in the *Stabat Mater* than the *Mouvements perpétuels*.

S.A. What led you to write religious music?

F.P. Heredity was deeply involved here. If one side of my art can be wholly explained by my mother's ultra-Parisian descent, you musn't forget that my father came from Aveyron, that sturdy, mountainous area between Auvergne and the Mediterranean basin. Poulenc, by the way, is a typical southern name. In architecture it is romanesque art—particularly the examples to be found in the south of France—that has always been my religious ideal, whether it's Vézelay, Autun, Moissac or Vierges du Puy or Conques. I like religious inspiration to express itself clearly in the sunshine with the same realism

Religious works; method of composing

as we can see on those romanesque capitals. My father, like all his family, was deeply religious but in a very liberal way, without the slightest meanness. At a time when I was seeking to drop roots into the very depths of my being, I composed my first religious work, *Les Litanies à la Vierge noire de Rocamadour*, parallel with my first songs to poems by Éluard.

S.A. So your first choral work was the *Litanies à la Vierge noire*?

F.P. Absolutely correct.

S.A. I wonder if that was the piece you got me to read one evening in the train from Bordeaux, where we'd met by chance. I can still remember your satisfaction when I said it seemed very beautiful and very pure to me.

F.P. That incident, which I recall very well, happened much later. It wasn't the *Litanies* but *Figure humaine*. I'm glad you've mixed up that big cantata for *a cappella* chorus with a religious work, and that you used the word "pure" which fits Paul Éluard's text so well. Isn't *Liberté*, which closes the work, a genuine litany? I wrote *Figure humaine* in a semi-religious mood, anyway. In 1943 so many people had just been imprisoned then deported and even shot, and you can imagine what it meant to me to see those grey-green uniforms marching through Paris. Finding in Éluard's poems the exact equivalent of what I felt, I set to work with complete faith, not without having commended my labours to Our Lady of Rocamadour. It's dedicated to Picasso, by the way. Its difficulty makes performances of it quite rare, unfortunately, but two years ago in New York I was able to see that, all topical considerations aside, it was capable of moving audiences who don't know—happily for them—what an "Occupation" means.

S.A. Don't you think your religious music could be related, in pictorial terms, to Mantegna and Zurbaran?

My Friends and Myself

F.P. Your compliment touches me, because Mantegna and Zurbaran correspond very closely, in fact, to my religious ideal. One with his mystical realism; the other with that ascetic purity of his, a purity that doesn't baulk, however, at dressing his women saints as fashionable ladies. Since my earliest childhood I've been passionately fond of painting. I owe it quite as many deep joys as music.

S.A. The pictures and drawings by Picasso, Braque, Matisse, Brianchon and Cocteau I've seen in your Paris home and at Noizay are proof of your wide taste. To my mind the sharp line of a Matisse, the healthy working-class happiness of a Dufy, correspond to the "popular" Poulenc, the ironical and tender Poulenc. On the other hand, Mantegna and Zurbaran evoke your religious music. As you very rightly said, it's romanesque, in the style of Mediterranean romanesque.

F.P. You're right. My Mass is much closer to Vittoria than to Josquin des Prés; it has a realistic side, if I may say so, which is characteristic of Mediterranean art.

S.A. We're beginning to pin down the character of Francis Poulenc and getting to know him well. But even so, we're not letting him off yet. What composers influenced your youth in music?

F.P. Without hesitation, Chabrier, Satie, Ravel and Stravinsky.

S.A. And who are your favourite composers?

F.P. I'm wildly eclectic. I like, in different degrees, of course, but with the same sincerity, Monteverdi, Scarlatti, Haydn, Mozart, Beethoven, Schubert, Chopin, Weber (my beloved Weber), Verdi, Mussorgsky, Debussy, Ravel, Bartók, and so on.

S.A. A like calls for its contrast: dislike. Are there any composers you can't bear?

Religious works; method of composing

F.P. Yes, Fauré. Of course, I realize he's a great composer, but some of his works like the Requiem make me curl up. They just affect me like that. Roussel for other reasons. I respect him, though he's personally opposed to me because of his harmonic sense, half-way between counterpoint and harmony, which is at the very farthest remove from what I like. By contrast, composers whose aesthetic is very different from mine, like Berg and Webern, I can get on with very well.

S.A. If you were sentenced to exile on a desert island, who are the five poets whose works you'd take with you?

F.P. Ronsard straight away, La Fontaine, Baudelaire, Apollinaire and Éluard. I only name French ones because poetry is untranslatable.

S.A. And your five composers?

F.P. Mozart before all else, then Schubert, Chopin, Debussy and Stravinsky.

S.A. Let's get back to dry land and finish our definition of you. What aesthetic do you follow, what's your philosophy of life?

F.P. You put me in a very difficult position to reply. I've not the slightest philosophical conception of life, because my outlook is too concrete to believe in speculations of the mind alone outside the religious faith which is instinctive and hereditary in me. As to my aesthetic, I have no preconceived idea. I compose as seems best to me when the wish takes me.

S.A. What's your method of working? What times and conditions are favourable to inspiration?

F.P. As I've already told you, Stéphane, I envy composers like Milhaud and Hindemith who can write wherever they may happen to be. I'm extremely susceptible visually, everything is an excuse for getting side-tracked, for frittering away

My Friends and Myself

my time. So I have to retire within myself and work in solitude. That's why I can't work in Paris, while by contrast I feel completely at ease in a hotel room with a piano. However, I need happy sights, because since I'm very prone to sadness I tend to create what I see out of my own feelings. My real time for working is in the morning. After seven in the evening, except for my work as a concert artist, I'm finished. On the other hand, it's joy for me to start work at six o'clock in the morning. As I've already told you, I work a lot at the piano, like Debussy, Stravinsky and so many others. Contrary to what is generally believed, I don't work easily. My first drafts, written in a sort of strange musical shorthand, are full of crossings-out. When a melodic idea presents itself to me in a certain key, I can only write it down (for the first time, of course) in that key. When I've told you that I've composed my least bad music between eleven o'clock and midday, I think I've told you everything.

II
My Friends

I

ERIK SATIE

Stéphane Audel. Where, how and when did you first know the composer of *Parade* and *Socrate*?

Francis Poulenc. I knew Satie in 1916 at my teacher's, Ricardo Viñes, the great Spanish pianist who was the first to play Debussy, Ravel, Falla and so many other composers. At that time I was working a lot at my piano playing, and if the classics were at the basis of Viñes' teaching, it didn't mean that Schumann excluded Satie from my lessons. Since 1910, a period when Satie began to be much talked about in Paris, I'd been fascinated by him. First by his amazing titles: *Morceaux en forme de poire* (Pieces in the shape of a pear), *Embryons desséchés* (Withered embryos), *Préludes flasques pour un chien* (Flabby preludes for a dog). Let's not forget I was then eleven years old. Suddenly music found a very real echo in me.

S.A. There's not the slightest doubt you were very heavily influenced by Erik Satie.

F.P. I don't deny it and I pride myself on it. So, in 1916, during my first year of study with Viñes, I had but one desire, to know Satie. I was then seventeen and eager for novelty. Stravinsky, whom I idolized and for whom my admiration is still intact, held no secrets for me: *L'Oiseau de feu*, *Petrouchka*, *Le Rossignol*, never left my piano. Of course, Debussy and

My Friends and Myself

Ravel were familiar to me down to the slightest details, but there you are, as always happens, those who followed them queered the pitch. The sub-standard Debussys and sub-standard Ravels had put me off. Only in passing, though, rest assured. They'd put me off certain fads, let's say mannerisms rather, of those two geniuses, and, as Picasso so rightly says: "Long live disciples! it's because of them that we go looking for something else." At the time I'd had my fill of whole-note scales, harp glissandos, muted horns, harmonics and quartets, just as brass, percussion and concerted pianos later turned us away from Stravinsky and so many of Hindemith's pranks. Look, every age has its little bad habits. You have to be a Webern to use false chromaticisms without creating in the hearer's mind an illusion of a systematic line of Russian mountains. Serial composition is the thing today [1956]. While we're waiting for the latest craze, let's come back to Satie. Everything I knew about Satie—and I did know everything— seemed to me to be tracing a new path for French music, such at least was my egoistical point of view as a future composer.

S.A. Do you think, then, that Satie opened up completely new horizons for you and many other young composers?

F.P. Without the slightest doubt. Of course, I won't say that all composers of my generation were influenced by Satie. Honegger, for example, escaped him completely, but Auric, Milhaud, Sauguet, me, we couldn't ignore him as a leader. Satie's case is, in fact, very strange, because he influenced directly or indirectly, by his music or his opinions, I mean, composers who were widely different, men like Debussy, Ravel, Stravinsky and many others. I've just told you that Honegger owes nothing to Satie, yet this didn't prevent him writing in *Incantations aux fossiles,* his book of criticism: "I have never been an admirer of Satie, but I am perfectly

Erik Satie

aware today of the timeliness of his views." Coming from an honest musician like Honegger, the judgement carries weight. You can't deny Satie's influence on Debussy. It also played the part of a happy chance in the birth of Pelléas et Mélisande. At the end of the nineteenth century Debussy and Satie met in Montmartre at the Auberge du Clou. They were fascinated by each other and that was the beginning of a long friendship. Debussy was then planning to set to music some Néri or other by that paltry writer Catulle Mendès, author of the libretto for Chabrier's Gwendoline,[1] and Satie immediately dissuaded him. He said: "Why shouldn't you set a Maeterlinck play?" Debussy chose Pelléas et Mélisande. So Satie is the wizard-godfather of that masterpiece.

S.A. Was the friendship that linked Satie and Debussy a long one?

F.P. I'll say so! It lasted for many years. Satie often lunched at Debussy's home in the avenue du Bois de Boulogne. Debussy liked Satie's gift of intuition, he liked his drollery, and neither could he remain untouched by his old friend's simple and very noble fellowship. You know the famous anecdote about Debussy reproaching Satie for his lack of form and Satie bringing him, some time later, the Morceaux en forme de poire for four hands, one piano. Some of his pieces, like the Préludes flasques pour un chien, are, do you see, a veiled and affectionate satire of certain rather pretentious titles of Debussy's Préludes, like La Terrasse des audiences du clair de lune... Did Debussy take the hidden reference badly? Was Satie unable to put up with Debussy's advice at a time when he himself was becoming famous? Whatever the true

---

[1] Mendès (1841-1909), a keen Wagnerian and author of a book on Wagner, wrote libretti for a number of composers. In 1891 he provided the text of Rodrigue et Chimène for Debussy, who, however, left this opera project uncompleted. [Translator.]

65

My Friends and Myself

facts are, in 1916 they quarrelled abruptly for ever, just as in 1924 and until his death Satie cut himself off from Auric and me as a result of aesthetic disagreements.

S.A. Now that's a problem in anecdotal history cleared up. Since you knew him so well, I'd like you to draw a portrait of Erik Satie.

F.P. H'mm! People who've been lucky enough to see Jean Cocteau's portraits of Satie can get an exact idea of him. For the benefit of others, I'll try to sketch the outlines of that strange character. Winter and summer alike, Satie never left off the bowler hat which he respected, nor the umbrella he adored. At his death, when people could at last get into his room at Arcueil where, during his lifetime, no one had ever dared venture, a hundred or so umbrellas were discovered . . . some of them weren't even taken out of the shop-paper they were wrapped up in. The reason why Auric one day heard the "bon Maître" calling him a blackguard, a ruffian, a foul scoundrel, was that quite by accident he'd stuck his umbrella into Satie's own. Satie's overcoat, rarely left off even in summer, wrapped him round like a dressing-gown. He had a goatee-beard which he carefully trimmed over and over again, and a pair of pince-nez which he was always re-adjusting with an imperious hand. Such were the characteristics of that odd half-French, half-Irish personality.[1] Satie had extremely clean personal habits. "I never take a bath," he'd say, "you can only wash properly in little bits! I use pumice stone on my skin; it goes farther than soap, dear lady," he explained one evening to an admirer of his. As the episode of Auric's umbrella shows, Satie's rages were fearsome, and so the quarrels that arose were painful. He rarely changed his mind once it was

---

[1] Poulenc makes a small slip here. Satie had Scottish ancestry through his mother, Jane Leslie Anton, who was born in London of Scottish parents. [Translator.]

Erik Satie

made up. He had something of a persecution mania, one must admit! After being very friendly with Ravel (it was Ravel who first played Satie's pieces at the Société de musique indépendante in 1911) Satie fell out so violently with him that he didn't hesitate to write in an avant-garde publication in 1920: "Maurice Ravel refuses the Légion d'Honneur . . . yet the whole of his work accepts it." We were probably wrong to follow him even in his aberrations, but we had at all costs to beware of Ravel's mirages. Later on Ravel was the first to forgive Auric and me our sins. And, do you see, even Stravinsky wasn't proof against receiving a jolt from Satie's aesthetic. After Stravinsky emerged from the sumptuous and barbaric atmosphere of *Les Noces*, the dry lucidity of Satie's *Parade* showed him another possible voice, that of *Mavra*, which was a very important turning point in the work of the Great Igor. And in one of Stravinsky's more recent works, the Sonata for two pianos, for example, there's a direct influence of Satie, first in the opening bars of the first movement, and then in the Andante there's a variation which is exactly in Satie's style.

S.A. How odd! After hearing your description one must agree that Satie was a picturesque character. Everyone knows he was very much of a night-bird, and in my mind I link him with another no less famous night-bird: Léon-Paul Fargue. Am I wrong, Francis?

F.P. Not a bit, you're not wrong at all. In fact, Satie and Fargue liked each other very much and went out a lot at night. Fargue is the only modern poet to have inspired Satie in a short song: *Les Ludions*, and especially in that masterpiece of a song, *La Statue de bronze*. It had a strong influence on my melodic style, and I cherish it with a secret love and endless gratitude. Let's come now to *Parade*, produced by Serge Diaghilev and the Russian Ballet. It marks a very important date

My Friends and Myself

from the musical and pictorial point of view, because, if Satie showed qualities of daring and innovation by introducing a typewriter into the orchestra, Diaghilev commissioned the first scenery Picasso ever did.

S.A. I think you were present at the first performance of *Parade*. I'd like you to tell me your memories of this.

F.P. *Parade* is, indeed, a landmark in the history of art. The collaboration, I nearly said conspiracy, between Cocteau, Satie and Picasso inaugurated the cycle of Diaghilev's great modern ballets. It wasn't only the typewriters in *Parade* that caused a scandal. Everything was new—plot, music, spectacle—and patrons who knew the Russian Ballet in the years before 1914 were astounded to see Picasso's curtain, which had already struck them as unusual, rising on Cubist scenery. It wasn't quite the frankly, strictly musical scandal of the *Sacre du printemps*. This time it was each of the arts throwing over the traces. And the production put on in 1917, in the middle of the war, struck some people as a challenge to good sense. Satie's music, so simple, so bare, so ingenuously clever, like a picture by the Douanier Rousseau, caused a scandal with its flippancy. For the first time—it's made up for it since—the music hall invaded art with a capital A. A one-step was danced in *Parade*. At that moment the house broke loose with hoots and applause. Up in the "Gods" the whole of Montparnasse was yelling: "Vive Picasso!" Auric, Roland-Manuel, Tailleferre, Durey and many other musicians bawled: "Vive Satie!" It was a fine scandal. Two figures stand out on the screen of my memories. One is Apollinaire in his officer's uniform with a bandage round his forehead . . . For him it was the triumph of his artistic beliefs. Another figure, very shadowed this time, is of Debussy, at the gates of death, leaving the auditorium and murmuring: "Perhaps! Perhaps! but I'm already too far away from all that!" After a period of unjust

Erik Satie

contempt, *Parade* now takes its place in the ranks of unquestioned masterpieces.

S.A. Let's talk now about Satie's greatest work. Talk to us about *Socrate*.

F.P. Oh, I won't say that *Socrate* is Satie's greatest work. I put it on an equal footing with *Parade*, though it's certainly his purest and most serious work. In 1917 the Princesse de Polignac, that irreplaceable patron who had just commissioned *Renard* from Stravinsky and *El retablo de Maese Pedro* from Falla, wanted to honour French music in the person of Satie. It was then that Satie got the idea of what he called "a musical reading". This he selected from among three extracts from Plato's *Dialogues* in Victor Cousin's translation and turned it into a sort of chamber cantata. In spite of the variety of the characters Satie never wanted but one singer, and not several, as people have wrongly said since. Satie, I repeat, set great importance on this impression of uniformity in the reading. Jane Bathori gave the first performance of this work, and since then Suzanne Balguerie, Marya Freund and Suzanne Danco have been the only ones to sing it in the true style. Just as Picasso was taking inspiration at the time from Ingres, Satie was looking for a new classicism and not the neo-classicism of a Stravinsky. With Satie there is never a return to anything; the music of *Socrate* is static by virtue of its purity, balance, reserve. The work is very difficult to sing because you risk confusing unity with monotony. I cannot myself hear the last section of the triptych, *La Mort de Socrate*, without a lump in the throat. I remember the first time it was played at the piano in Adrienne Monnier's famous Paris bookshop: Gide, Claudel, Valéry, Fargue, Picasso, Braque, Derain, Stravinsky and many others had come to listen to the strange message of the Sage of Arcueil! All of them were struck in varying degrees and at different levels by that lesson in greatness and honesty which makes *Socrate* a masterpiece. Unfortunately there is no record of it available.

S.A. What you've just said on this point is very interesting, Francis. And when you talk of that gathering at Adrienne Monnier's, it takes on a legendary appearance today: Gide, Claudel . . . Valéry, Picasso, quite extraordinary. But I'd like to ask you a question now about Erik Satie's piano work. I know the importance you attach to it. Your own talent as a pianist and the wealth of music you've written for the piano lead me to suppose you're talking of Satie rather in the way a virtuoso appraises the talents of another, for I'd imagine that Satie, like you, was a pianist, wasn't he?

F.P. Oh no, not at all.

S.A. Really?

F.P. Satie played the piano very badly, especially towards the end of his life. He was very fond of the piano for sure, but most of his pieces were written on café tables at Arcueil Cachan. Anyway, the only piano to be found in Satie's home after his death was completely unplayable, and Braque bought it as a relic, nothing more. But often, during his morning visits to Cocteau's, Milhaud's, Auric's or my home, he would mutter into his beard, half-ironically, half-seriously: "Mon vieux, could I try out some little thing?" Then he would take out of his pocket music exercise-books such as schoolboys use and dazzle us with his extraordinary inspiration. Satie's piano music isn't appreciated at its real value, probably because of his titles . . . obviously it's off-putting to see, printed in programmes: *Aperçus désagréables* (Unpleasant glimpses), *Danse de travers* (Crooked dance), *Airs à faire fuir* (Airs to put to flight), etc. Yet what wonderful music! ! ! Let's take as an example the *Descriptions automatiques* for piano. These are three short pieces. The first, *Sur un bateau* is a sort of ironical pitching to a tango rhythm. The second, which is called *Sur une*

Erik Satie

lanterne, has the poetry of a garden at night painted by Bonnard. And the last piece, *Sur un casque,* is in the best style of the Douanier Rousseau: anniversary of the taking of the Bastille, the carmagnole, and so on. You must forget the farcical literature that surrounds these tiny pieces, let yourself go, and their charm will work.

2

MAX JACOB

Stéphane Audel.

> Je l'ai vu sur les quais d'Ouchy
> Par un temps radieux et fade
> Il contemplait d'un air maussade
> Les bons Suisses endimanchés
> Ganté de noir, de noir vêtu
> Il semblait confit en vertu
> Mais sous sa paupière bistrée
> Crépitait un regard d'almée.
> A son crâne nu comme un bol
> Le ciel faisait une auréole
> Digne des martyrs et des saints
> Je le saluai à dessein
> Car noble et pauvre comme Job
> J'avais reconnu Max Jacob.[1]

Since we're going to talk about Max Jacob, I thought I'd dedicate those lines to him, unworthy as they are of the strange and wonderful talent of the poet who wrote *Le Cornet à dés*, the *Laboratoire central*, and *Les Pénitents en maillot rose*. I'm

---

[1] I saw him on the jetties at Ouchy / In bright insipid weather / He was looking in a sulky sort of way / At the worthy Swiss in their Sunday best / Black gloved, dressed in black / He seemed steeped in virtue / But under his swarthy eyelid / Sparkled the mischievous look of a dancing girl. / Around his cranium bare as a basin / The sky made a halo / Worthy of martyrs and saints / I greeted him deliberately / For noble and poor as Job / I had recognized Max Jacob.

Max Jacob

aware, Francis, that you knew Max Jacob well. Would you like to tell us when and under what circumstance you met him?

Francis Poulenc. When you met Max Jacob at Ouchy it was certainly at the end of his life, when he came to visit his old friend, Liane de Pougy, Princesse Ghyka, who died in Lausanne. The friendship between that famous beauty of the nineteen-hundreds and Max Jacob was very touching. One was the Venus of harlotry, the other of Bohemianism, and both of them presented the spectacle of a life ending in simple and exemplary fashion. That's what brought them together. But let's get back to Max Jacob. I knew him a very, very long time ago, in 1917. It was the year of the great scandals in the arts. The 1914 war so little resembled our present wars that at only fifty miles from the German lines Paris was in a ferment about the famous Picasso-Matisse exhibition, the first performance of *Parade* or the première of Apollinaire's *Les Mamelles de Tirésias*. By the way, Max Jacob sang in the unbelievable choruses of *Les Mamelles*, in an unbelievable voice . . . I must say. A keen admirer since childhood of every branch of poetry, I admired unreservedly that astonishing work by Max Jacob: *Le Cornet à dés*, which I hold to be one of the three masterpieces among French prose-poems. The two others are Baudelaire's *Le Spleen de Paris* and Rimbaud's *Saison en enfer*. That strange miscellany is at the source of a whole poetic style in French, one that's given birth to surrealism and, at a very much lower level, Jacques Prévert. Apollinaire's reputation, so well justified, has often eclipsed Max Jacob's; they influenced each other in turn, like Picasso and Braque, between the years 1911 and 1913. I'd like to tell you the story of my first visit to Max Jacob. Raymond Radiguet, "a child with a big stick", as Max Jacob used to say of him, took me to see Max at home one morning because he knew I liked him. Doubtless our past always takes on magic colours, yet I don't think I'm misleading

My Friends and Myself

you when I say that that first visit to Max Jacob, with the author of *Le Diable au corps*, is one of the dearest memories of my life. Radiguet was then living in the eastern suburb of Paris at Joinville on the banks of the Marne, those banks he's described so well in *Le Diable au corps* and which form a part of my own youth. We had agreed to meet at a café in the Place de la Bastille at ten o'clock in the morning. As if it were yesterday I can see Radiguet still, wearing a sort of felt Panama hat too large for him, (perhaps it was his father's) with the inevitable stick that was too big for him in his hand. We jumped into a taxi for Montmartre where Max lived at the time, a few steps away from Sacré-Coeur in the rue Gabrielle. The decayed house was like the ones you see in films about Montmartre or in those little genre pictures that are still sold in the Place du Tertre. Max lived in a big, very dark room on the ground floor. A mirror-fronted cupboard without a back took up the middle of the room, you stepped through it as you would a door, which made Max say comically: "Here's my drawing-room, there's my bedroom." Max had a habit of literally deluging you with compliments which he handed out indiscriminately while thinking about something else. So, affectionate, voluble and smiling, he told us of his happiness at receiving a novelist of genius and a "tremendous" musician! Just that! (Radiguet was fifteen years old, I was eighteen!) You can imagine the scene!!! A bit taken aback, even though I'd been warned, I couldn't prevent myself blushing like a peony. Radiguet, who was used to it, carried on: "What's new, Max?" "People don't like me," groaned Max, "Apollinaire is the only one they approve of. Do you know what Picasso said to Modigliani the other day? Yes, yes, yes, I know perfectly well, Reverdy was there . . ." And he launched into a string of gossip that mortified and delighted him at the same time. In those days, dressed in alpaca, Max looked like the sexton from the Basilica of Montmartre. I told you last

Max Jacob

time about a whimsical creature: Erik Satie. I swear that Max yielded nothing to him in oddness.

S.A. Were Picasso, Derain, Braque and Modigliani all living in Montmartre still at that time?

F.P. No, no, no, no, the great exodus had already taken place; the time of the "Bateau lavoir", the nickname of an old Montmartre house where so many painters and writers lived, was over. Picasso, Derain, Juan Gris and many others had left Montmartre; that was the origin of the famous Montparnasse of 1918, the Saint-Germain-des-Prés of the post-war years. Only Braque, in his studio in the rue Caulaincourt, and Max in the rue Gabrielle, stayed faithful to Montmartre. In those days Picasso lived near the Montparnasse cemetery, Derain in the rue Bonaparte, and Gris and Modigliani near the boulevard Montparnasse.

S.A. And do you know why Max Jacob didn't follow his friends when they left Montmartre for Montparnasse?

F.P. Listen, Stéphane, I think, in all sincerity, it was the closeness of Sacré-Coeur that kept Max in the rue Gabrielle until his first departure for the abbey of Saint-Benoît-sur-Loire. In spite of his wildness and the fleeting blasphemies of his conversation, Max had been a believer for a very long time, and his end proved it, anyway.

S.A. Are you referring to the story Max wrote about the second appearance of Christ replacing a crime film on a cinema screen? . . .

F.P. That story may seem at first glance a very literary one, but it's no less true that Max was, at the time of his first conversion, a profound believer, and you can be certain of it. The conversion goes back, in fact, to his youth.

S.A. Yes, his conversion, as you say, or rather his illumina-

My Friends and Myself

tion, does indeed date from 7th October, 1919. He was young at the time!

F.P. That day Christ appeared to him on the wall of the room he occupied in the rue Ravignan. He has spoken in terms worthy of Pascal about the dazzling brightness of his vision. However, in spite of his keenness and his faith, Max was to wait until 18th February, 1915, to be baptized. On the evening of his baptism he had a second vision, and this time in fact, as you've just said, in a way and a place unexpected: in a cinema, on the screen.

S.A. Here is how he talks of it:

> Je prends à témoin, Seigneur, qui m'a mis à neuf
> Mon âme de pécheur rempli de turpitudes;
> Tu sais de quels péchés j'avais pris l'habitude,
> Dans quel gâchis je vivais, tu sais dans quel enfer,
> Quelles résolutions ta visite a fait naître
> Dans le chrétien que, grâce à toi et aux bons prêtres,
> Me voici devenu, plein de sens et de raison.
> Donc, la première fois, tu vins dans ma maison.
> Et la seconde fois au Cinématographe ...
> "Vous allez donc alors au Cinématographe,
> Me dit un confesseur, la mine confondue,
> —Eh, mon Père! Le Seigneur n'y est-il pas venu?"[1]

S.A. Obviously the comic Max is showing the cloven hoof here!

F.P. Yes, yes, but it's wonderful!

---

[1] O Lord, who hast renewed me, I take as witness / My sinner's soul filled with vileness; / Thou knowest what sins I had got the habit of, / In what mire I lived, Thou knowest what hell, / What resolves Thy visit has given birth to / In the Christian whom, thanks to Thee and Thy good priests, / I am now become, full of good sense and reason. / So, the first time, Thou cam'st into my house. / And the second time at the pictures ... / "So you go to the pictures," / Said a confessor to me, discountenanced, / —Well, Father! Didn't the Lord come there?"

Max Jacob

S.A. He often showed it, one must say, because the great mystical outpourings were followed by little poems of this nature:

> Loïe Fuller c'est épatant
> Sur le bi, sur le bout, sur le bi du bout du banc . . .
> Mais ce Rodin est un salaud,
> C'est zéro!
> Otero.
> Ah! voilà un numéro![1]

There's enough there to silence those who gave credit to his conversion . . . One has to say it . . .

F.P. It's inspired . . . you know. That Rimbaud poem where Camembert comes into it?

S.A. Yes, yes, that's true, it's a bit in the same vein.

F.P. There's a link between everything, whether in music or poetry. Obviously one may be surprised by the tone of that conversion, and the faith may have seemed like a literary attitude for quite some time, but whoever saw Max living in the monastery of Saint-Benoît-sur-Loire cannot doubt its genuineness. There were some who spitefully wanted it to be believed that Max Jacob had left Paris solely through lack of money and not through devotion, which isn't correct; Max wasn't rolling in money, of course, but, as they say, he got by with selling delightful gouaches, sometimes with Breton subjects, sometimes Parisian, to collectors. No, if Max left Paris for Saint-Benoît, it was genuinely to avoid temptations which he described as traps of the devil. "At Saint-Benoît," Max wrote to me, "I have less opportunity to sin; a bit of backbiting, of course, but subjects for backbiting are so limited! Naturally,

---

[1] As Poulenc remarked earlier, poetry is untranslatable, and this particular piece of sprightly nonsense, which depends on the very language itself for its wit, cannot be satisfactorily expressed in English. [Translator.]

I've been able to say that the grocer's wife . . . and the commercial traveller in 'Lion Noir' polish . . . But ssh! . . . I'll be quiet! . . ."

S.A. There's the whole of Max Jacob in that remark! It's irresistible!

F.P. I quote the letter from memory, but I'm sure of the content . . . sure of it!

S.A. Was his life at Saint-Benoît-sur-Loire very edifying?

F.P. Definitely!

S.A. But then society wanted him back from time to time, high society even, isn't that true, Francis?

F.P. Indeed yes. When Max came to Paris it was like a soldier on leave. After a few days he'd say: "I must get back again. I feel I'm going to the bad!" All the same, he came up to Paris a lot, and then he left Saint-Benoît-sur-Loire. He lived for three or four years at least in Paris, in the Hôtel Nollet, in Montmartre, or rather in Batignolles, around 1935. And it was at that point that he set off again once and for all to Saint-Benoît, that he never left it again.

S.A. But before talking about the Max Jacob of Saint-Benoît-sur-Loire, let's return, if you'll allow, to the comic and fanciful Max, the Max who used to frequent the Restaurant Vernin, of which he said:

> Ça m'embête d'aller chez Vernin,
> mais il faut y aller quand même
> car on y prend des verres nains
> et des fromages à la crème![1]

[1] It's a bore going to Vernin's / but I must go there just the same / because you drink from dwarf glasses / and eat cream cheeses! The point lies in the witty rhyme of 'Vernin' and 'verres nains'. [Translator.]

Max Jacob

That unpublished quatrain corresponds to the Parisian Max whose memory, Francis, I'd like you to talk about . . . Will you?

F.P. There's nothing easier. Let's see now, in the album of my memories of Max I'd choose, I must say . . . something really out-and-out, I'd choose that strange evening when Cécile Sorel had decided to bring Marcel Proust and Max Jacob together at the dinner table. Lucien Daudet, Alphonse Daudet's son and Léon's brother, was the ringleader in that adventure. There was, let's see, it was in 1925 . . . There was a very smart night-club, "Le jardin de ma soeur", a few steps away from the Opéra, where fashionable Paris came to quench the passion for dancing that possessed it from 1918 onwards. Max Jacob having said during lunch at Madame Alphonse Daudet's that he'd like to meet Proust, Cécile Sorel, who was present at that lunch, caught the ball on the rebound and said: "Ah, my dear great poet, we'll arrange it, shan't we, Lucien?" Lucien Daudet was a close friend of Marcel Proust and undertook to carry out negotiations, because there was a very ceremonious, ambassadorial side to Proust. At that time Proust was ailing more and more, went out very sparingly and very late at night, when his chronic asthma gave him a bit of rest. To tell the truth, in fact, it was realized later that Proust, knowing his days were numbered, shut himself up most of all so that he could work feverishly on the end of his book. At last Proust accepted Sorel's invitation and we fixed the date for a Saturday evening. I can see our table again with Sorel crowned with feathers and literally bound up in strings of pearls, Lucien phlegmatic and very spruce, Jacques Porel, Réjane's witty son, the master of ceremonies on this occasion, Georges Auric and me, astonished and delighted, and Max wearing a frock coat with velvet collar that made him look like a provincial headmaster. "Do you like dancing, dear poet?" cooed Sorel. "Good heavens, Madame! . . ." And before we could get over our astonishment, Cécile Sorel and Max Jacob were waltzing in the middle of the dance floor. When the dance was over, Max, taking his seat, whispered in my ear: "Oh bless my soul—I wanted to take Holy Communion this morning!" That's typical Max Jacob. Proust telephoned very late from the Ritz Hotel apologizing for being too exhausted to join us. I don't know, however, if Max and Proust ever met later on, though I don't personally think they did . . .

S.A. No, neither do I, I've never heard they did. Perhaps . . . I don't know . . .

F.P. It's not important.

S.A. All the same, it's a wonderful adventure.

F.P. Yes, it was fun.

S.A. Quite unexpected, I must say. But let's turn serious again, Francis. Did you often collaborate with Max Jacob?

F.P. Oh yes, of course. In 1931 I composed a cycle of five songs to some of his poems in the Breton style, but notably in 1932 I composed, I dare to say so immodestly, one of my most significant works: *Le Bal masqué*, a secular cantata for baritone and chamber orchestra.

S.A. Aren't they the burlesque poems Max dedicated to you in *Les Pénitents en maillot rose*?

F.P. No, no, not at all; the poems you refer to are the ones Max wrote for me in 1921, which I set to music, dedicated to Darius Milhaud, and later destroyed. No, no, no, no, the poems in *Le Bal Masqué* appeared in the collection called *Le Laboratoire central*. Their violence, their truculence, their whimsicality attracted me then. I found in them that "tuppence coloured" quality of the pictures in the Paris weeklies of my youth, and from there was born that odd musical carnival I've

Max Jacob

always prized greatly. It's like the Mamelles de Tirésias for me, do you understand?

S.A. I'd like to ask you a question: have you any unpublished poems by Max Jacob?

F.P. Yes, I've two charming unpublished pieces. The first is called Le Jardin demandé (The garden asked for). Here it is:

> Le vent qui souffle a fait tomber les pommes
> Et les gamins courent les ramasser
> Les bras croisés, Monsieur l'Abbé bougonne
> C'est la rançon, France, de tes péchés
> Mes haricots c'était mon espérance
> Mais nous n'avons pas eu d'eau cet été
> Les blés sont secs, oh! malheureuse France
> Pour du raisin, on en aura, oui, certes
> Du vin, bien sûr, pour achever ta perte
> Mais voyez donc les fleurs de mon jardin
> Et même pas de vert pour mes lapins!
> Et même pas et même pas de vert pour mes lapins![1]

S.A. It's quite charming!

F.P. It's a charming poem, which it's quite impossible to set to music, however. Some days afterwards, and this is very significant as far as Max is concerned, he sent me the following letter with a new poem:

> Mon Francis,
> Je préfère que tu déchires la pièce où parle mon curé
> Si le hasard la lui faisait connaître, il pourrait s'en formaliser

---

[1] The wind that blows has tumbled the apples / And the youngsters run and pick them up / His arms crossed, Monsieur l'Abbé grumbles / This is the ransom, France, of your sins / My beans were my hope / But we've had no rain this summer / The corn is dry, oh! unhappy France / Assuredly we shall have grapes, oh yes, / And wine, of course, to finish off your ruin / But behold the flowers in my garden / And there's not even greenery for my rabbits / And not even, not even greenery for my rabbits!

My Friends and Myself

De plus, je ne juge pas digne
Quand on habite une maison
De faire des pièces malignes
Contre les gens qui nous y ont.
Déchire donc, Francis, déchire!
Voici un morceau plus joli
Il est plus poétique
Et puis surtout il est plus poli.
Je t'aime mon cher musicien,
Pourquoi le dire tu le sais bien, Max.[1]

And then, at the bottom, he's added: "You can check that the letter's in verse."

S.A. Indeed it's in verse, and charming verse at that.

F.P. There was a new poem with it, which I haven't set to music either, but which is delightful. Here it is:

>   *Tableau mécanique à musique*
> Ah que tout me semble facile
> Quand j'habite votre maison
> J'entends votre rouet qui file,
> Le puits gémir sous le balcon
> Je vois un coquelicot dans l'herbe,
> Fleurir les blés chez le voisin
> Et par-dessus le mur, les gerbes
> Sur des chars et, sur le chemin,
> J'entends le batelier qui passe,
> Des cris d'oiseaux, d'enfants joyeux,
> J'aperçois aussi dans ma glace

---

[1] My Francis,
I'd prefer you to tear up the piece in which my *curé* speaks / If by chance he got to know of it, he might take objection / What's more, I don't think it proper / When you live in a house / To write mischievous things / About the people who have you there. / So tear it up, Francis, tear it up! / Here's a prettier piece / It's more poetic / And, too, it's more polite above all. / I love you my dear musician, / Why bother to say so since you know it well, Max.

Max Jacob

Votre cou blanc, vos jolis yeux,
Et votre main qui semble lasse.
Hôtesse où peut-on être mieux.[1]

S.A. It's absolutely delightful.

F.P. Very pretty, but impossible to set to music.

S.A. Perhaps, but it's charming.

F.P. It's very precious ... It belongs among my relics.

S.A. Look after them well because they're worth the trouble. But in the end, so much fantasy, freshness and purity led Max Jacob to a very lonely, unjust and cruel end. Just now you referred to his life at Saint-Benoît, to his devotion. I'd like to ask you if you saw Max again during the Occupation.

F.P. I saw him again but once in 1942 during a brief stay he made in Paris with his incomparable friend Pierre Colle, the Paris picture dealer, who died an untimely death—he was a great friend and I was very fond of him. He was a friend of Derain, Georges Auric ... I hadn't seen Max for a very long time and he seemed to me deeply changed, physically quite as much as morally. He was obsessed by the Jewish persecutions carried out by the German occupation and you'd have thought he felt himself lost already! Physically Max closely resembled his mother as I saw her once in Quimper running her antique shop. It was at Quimper, in fact, that Max was born. In 1929, knowing I was going to Brittany, Max said to me: "Please go and see my mother. You'll find her in the window. Be sure to tell her," he added, (half-serious, half-joking), "that I'm some-

---

[1] *Mechanical music table*
How easy it all seems to me / When I live in your house / I hear your spinning wheel turn, / The well murmur beneath the balcony / I see a poppy in the grass, / The wheat flourishing in your neighbour's field / And above the wall, sheaves / On carts and, on the way, / I hear the boatman pass, / Cries of birds and merry children, / I see too in my glass / Your white neck, your pretty eyes, / And your hand that seems wearied. / Hostess, where else could one be more content?

body VERRRY famous and VERRRY respected in Paris. It's useless to refer to anyone, she doesn't know who Claudel is, or Monsieur Paul Valéry." On arriving in Quimper, I didn't neglect to visit Madame Jacob, whom I did indeed find in the window, like a waxwork at Madame Tussaud's. She was mixed up in a collection of strange objects and spent long days watching passers-by in the street from her window. Even when Max was old he feared this odd person, who at bottom wasn't so terrible as all that. Somebody said very comically that Max wanted to do everything like Apollinaire, who had a dreadful mother.

S.A. Yes, a terrifying mother.

F.P. Somebody said—I can't remember if it was Reverdy or another—"Max talks like that about his mother because he wants to be like Apollinaire." In reality Madame Jacob was a very worthy woman!

S.A. She had nothing of the dragon about her, in short.

F.P. Fear, d'you see, fear of displeasing Picasso, fear of quarrelling with Breton and Éluard, fear of Reverdy, fear of Cocteau; fear was one of the fundamentals of Max's character. Alas, in 1942 his fears were only too well justified. Anyway, Max felt it. He had only one anxiety: to get back to Saint-Benoît-sur-Loire, where he thought there was more safety. In fact the monks liked him very much, and his little quarters in the monastery seemed like a quiet burrow for the unfortunate hare. In the opinion of everyone around him during those awful Occupation years, Max's devotion was exemplary, which was a great comfort for him as it was for those who were close to him. Of his own volition he insisted on wearing the yellow star.[1] We thought that down there on the banks of

---

[1] In occupied France the Germans ordered all Jews to wear a distinguishing yellow star as a further Teutonic refinement of humiliation. [Translator.]

the Loire nothing could happen to him. Alas, we were deceived, and a very short time before the Liberation of Paris he was arrested by the Gestapo and taken to Drancy on the outskirts of the city. Notified immediately by the monks of Saint-Benoît, his Parisian friends did everything to save him. The painter José-Maria Sert, as a Spaniard, was easily able to get an order freeing him, but when that order arrived at Drancy Max was at death's door. He was dying from pneumonia contracted during his transfer from Saint-Benoît to Paris.

S.A. It's dreadful.

F.P. He had the consolation of finding at Drancy, as a Red Cross nurse, one of our friends, Mlle Yvonne Franck, who was leading dancer at the Opéra. It was from her that we had all the details of Max's death. It's obvious, unquestionable, that Max died a saint. He spoke, it seems, very softly: "I'm not afraid!", for on the threshold of death he believed more than ever in a better world where the injustices of his sad life would be righted. Max is often painted in ludicrous colours, but one last time, a short while before his death, he portrayed himself, in overwhelming fashion, wearing his poor yellow star. It's in a last prose poem entitled: *Love of one's neighbour*. It's a very moving poem. It proves that Max was a great-hearted man, a very sensitive man.

S.A. And modest.

F.P. And modest, oh very much so! Here's the prose poem:

Love of one's neighbour
Who saw the toad cross a street? He's a very little fellow: a doll couldn't be tinier. He crawls along on his knees: would you say he was ashamed . . . ? No! he's rheumatic, one leg drags behind, he brings it forward! where is he going like this? He comes out of the drain, poor clown. No one has noticed this toad in the street.

My Friends and Myself

Once upon a time people didn't notice me in the street, now children laugh at my yellow star. Happy toad! you haven't got a yellow star.[1]

It's an astonishing poem because it reveals Max's intimate side.

S.A. The humble side.

F.P. I've tried to read it to you as he read his poems, because when you read Max Jacob's poems you have to bring out the grotesque and comic side as much as the poetic and human. There. That's all I have to tell you about Max.

[1] *Derniers poèmes en vers et en prose*, Éditions Gallimard.

3

MANUEL DE FALLA

Stéphane Audel. So far we've spoken of Erik Satie and Max Jacob. We've highlighted the duality of the poet and the musician, and especially their mysticism. Platonist with Satie and Christian with Jacob, but as genuinely sincere with one as with the other. I warn you now that today I'm going to question you about the mysticism of Manuel de Falla. This may seem disconcerting, because after all Falla remains for most people the wonderful magician of legendary Spain, the Spain of *El amor brujo, La vida breve* and *El sombrero de tres picos*. It's a Spain that's very far away from the land of Teresa of Avila or Ignatius de Loyola. Every Spaniard carries a fund of great religious fervour within him, but I'd like you to explain the reasons which make you say Falla was a great mystic.

Francis Poulenc. Well, to start a discussion of Falla by way of his mysticism is to take the subject at its highest level. Still, I don't mind such an abrupt approach and I gladly agree to it. First of all, let's say there's no more violently contradictory country than Spain. They pray to the Madonna with all their strength, burn a forest of candles, and then go out and kill their rivals. Obviously, what people are wrong to think is that Spain is nothing but sun, oranges, guitars, mantillas, pomegranate flowers. As in bull-fighting, the ring is divided into two sections: *sol* and *sombra*. There's a Spain that's *sol* and a Spain that's *sombra*. These two sections are often mixed together in an unexpected way. Now Stéphane, you've just spoken of Saint Teresa of Avila. Well, did you know that Saint Teresa ordered her Carmelites, for the health of their soul and body, to dance to the sound of the guitar and castanets? The Spanish Carmelites have respected the tradition ever since. In a recent French translation of Saint Teresa's *Book of Foundations* you can admire Madame Yvonne Chevalier's very fine photographs. Inside the convent, by special authorization of Rome, you can see young Carmelites dancing with castanets in hand to the sound of the prior's guitar. Once you've established this principle of contrasts you can more easily admit that Falla's mysticism stands side by side with his picturesqueness. What is particularly admirable in Falla is that his picturesque quality is never on the surface, as it is with the painter Zuloga, but is a part of his being, as with Goya. Yes, Falla was a great mystic, and the final picture of him that remains with me is that of a man, or rather a Zurbaran monk, praying in a church in Venice.

S.A. Venice?

F.P. Yes, Venice, because it was in Venice that I saw Falla for the last time, in September 1932. I'd come to Venice for the first performance of my Concerto for two pianos which I played with Jacques Février and the orchestra of La Scala, Milan. The work had been commissioned from me by the Princesse Edmond de Polignac I've already talked about. That great lady, who was American by origin (her father was the Singer who invented sewing machines), was an enlightened patron all her life. She was the friend of Chabrier, Fauré, Ravel, Richard Strauss, Stravinsky, Satie and also Falla, from whom she commissioned *El retablo de Maese Pedro*. I lived that month of September with Falla in the Palazzo Polignac on the Grand Canal; Artur Rubinstein and other artists lived there too. The large drawing-rooms were filled with pianos. At one

Manuel de Falla

of those pianos Fauré had once composed his famous so-called "Venice" songs which he dedicated to the Princesse. What a lot of music we made in 1932! I remember, among others, a morning when I played for Falla, at two pianos with Artur Rubinstein, the *Noches en los jardines de España*; Artur, of course, played the piano solo while I played the orchestral part. Because Falla had always showed me as much kindness as affection from the beginning, we were very happy to meet again under such circumstances. At that Venice Festival they were giving a stage performance of the *Retablo*: Falla and I set off early each morning for rehearsals, all the earlier because they were preceded for Falla by daily Mass. I'd be telling a lie if I said that I myself was as faithful to Mass. When I didn't go there with Falla I'd join him in a café near the Teatro del Fenice where he had breakfast after Communion. By contrast with Max Jacob whom I talked to you about the other evening, Falla never spoke of his faith.

S.A. Never?

F.P. No, never. He lived it intensely and secretly. In a little Venetian café one morning Falla talked to me at length about Pedrell, a Spanish composer little known outside Spain, who played a considerable part in Falla's musical development when he left for Madrid in 1914. The war called him back to Madrid. Falla always said that he'd rediscovered Spain in music through Debussy, but, on returning to his country, he realized from his contact with Pedrell that there were other sources of inspiration for a musician apart from Madrid zarzuelas, and that's where he's quite different from Albéniz.

S.A. Yes, it's not well enough known.

F.P. People don't take it into consideration enough. It's obviously a cultural difference. Falla was closer to folklore, Albéniz to the zarzuela. In those four volumes of his, the *Cancionero popular español*, Felipe Pedrell did for folklore and

My Friends and Myself

old Spanish music what Bartók did for Hungarian popular song, that is, they both gave definitive form to an authentic tradition of their country. You'll come across an echo of Pedrell's very characteristic harmonization in the Fisherman's Song in Falla's El *amor brujo*, and even more so in the *Retablo*. There was something secret and confidential in Falla's conversation! He very rarely gave his opinion of other contemporary works. He liked or didn't like, and that was it! Let's say, rather, that he admired or despised, because that was more in his nature as a proud and secret man. With him, technical details were rarely emphasized; and Heaven knows what a technique he had! They said he was mysterious and nothing could be more incorrect, because Falla was a mystic in the pure state, limpid, on the contrary, like a piece of crystal. He had some very amusing sides, however. During rehearsals he never got angry, he became nervy! I've known this type of Spanish nerviness with my master Ricardo Viñes, too. All at once, in both men, their speech took on the rhythm of a guitar peevishly tuning up!

S.A. Tock tock tock tock! Absolutely, I can hear it this very moment.

F.P. And, on the contrary, what serenity when Falla touched on the spiritual plane! I'd like to picture here one of the rarest, most wonderful days I've ever lived. Think of Falla and me staying alone one afternoon in the Palazzo Polignac; all the other guests had gone off by water to the Lido. Towards five o'clock in the afternoon I suggested a little walk to Falla and we set off through the maze of Venetian alleyways where you can lose yourself so easily. Although my sense of direction is uncertain, I succeeded in finding a wonderful little church where I'd been several days before and where there was a magnificent organ. Today I've forgotten the name of that little church, but I swear to you, Stéphane, that I wouldn't take

Manuel de Falla

long to pick it out if I landed in Venice! Now, it was the time of Benediction. The church was hung with red damask for some festival or other. There was an overpowering smell of incense and tuberoses that made your temples throb. The organist seemed as if he was playing some of Frescobaldi's music, and that very purely, for us alone. As soon as we'd entered the church Falla sank down in prayer, and just as they tell of certain saints who in ecstasy suddenly vanish from the sight of the profane, so I had the impression of losing Falla. After a long minute or so, having decided to go, I approached him and tapped him on the shoulder. He looked at me for a moment without seeing me and then plunged into his prayer again! I went out of the church and have never seen Falla since, because that very evening he took the train, while I was rehearsing at the Teatro del Fenice. Falla was going back to Spain at that time . . . and only left it again at the Civil War to reach Argentina. So I never saw him again. For me, that final vision of a composer I've always loved and always admired . . . it was like an Assumption!

S.A. You're not mistaken, Falla did end his life in Argentina in the little town of Cordoba. He lived there like a saint—so I've been told—and already out of this world, so to say. When I stayed myself in Buenos Aires, Argentinian musicians told me that Falla was living on his own in a sort of contemplative state, you might say even that he obeyed the rules of a hermit's life, which supports, you see, your opinion of him. But tell me, I'd like to know, when and how you first knew Manuel de Falla.

F.P. Since I must always tell you where and when I knew my friends, here we go: I met Falla in 1918 when he came back to Paris after the 1914 war. I knew him at Ricardo Viñes' place—Viñes, as you know, was the dedicatee of the *Noches en los jardines de España*, and I saw a lot of him later on in

My Friends and Myself

Russian Ballet circles. It was the time when Diaghilev, Falla and Picasso were preparing the excellent *Sombrero de tres picos*.

S.A. But Falla had already lived in Paris before the 1914 war, hadn't he?

F.P. For many a year, I think! Falla came to Paris in 1907 and only left it finally because of the 1914 war. Paris was where he studied and Paris was where he knew Debussy, Dukas, Schmitt, who became his great friends.

S.A. And doubtless Maurice Ravel?

F.P. Yes, Ravel... naturally. But let's not forget that Falla was Debussy's close friend and that relations between Debussy and Ravel weren't always very warm!

S.A. Yes, that's true...

F.P. That state of affairs was due to the Debussyites and Ravellians more than to the composers themselves! It was Debussy who first sensed Falla's genius, and it was thanks to Debussy that his early works were published in Paris. Thanks, too, to Paul Dukas that the Opéra at Nice and then the Paris Opéra-Comique did *La vida breve*.

S.A. Do you think Debussy exercised any influence on Falla?

F.P. Without a doubt. Indeed, those two masters were made to understand and admire each other, and their friendship was unclouded. Falla was terribly sad at Debussy's death. And that was the moment when he dedicated to the great Frenchman's memory that admirable *Homenaje* for guitar, where at the end, by quoting two bars from *Soirée dans Grenade*, Falla pays his respects to Debussy, who, as I told you just now, by his own avowal, had shown him the way to Spain in music.

S.A. But you yourself have dedicated your trio for piano, oboe and bassoon to Manuel de Falla, haven't you?

Francis Poulenc as a small boy

Schoenberg and Poulenc, Vienna, 1922

"Les Six".

L to R: standing, Francis Poulenc, Germaine Tailleferre, Georges Auric, Louis Durey; seated, Arthur Honegger, Jean Cocteau, Darius Milhaud

Stravinsky

Erik Satie in middle age

Pierre Bernac and Francis Poulenc on their return from the USA, 1949

Suzanne Peignot, the favourite singer of his early songs, with Poulenc

Denise Duval in *Les Mamelles de Tirésias*

Max Jacob and Lucien Daudet

Paul Éluard, by Picasso

Léon-Paul Fargue, Maurice Ravel, Georges Auric, Paul Morand

Francis Poulenc at Noizay

Manuel de Falla

F.P. I have. In 1925 I dedicated that little trio to Falla to show him as best I could my loving admiration.

S.A. Tell me, Francis, did Debussy visit Falla in Spain?

F.P. Oh no, by no means. I don't think Debussy ever got farther into Spain than San Sebastian. He sensed Spain, with his inspired flair and also his knowledge of Albéniz, whom he admired. In Debussy's time, actually, there was no folk song available on gramophone records and very few folk song publications even. So Debussy sensed and guessed at Spain. *La Puerta del vino*, the piano prelude, was written on receiving a picture postcard Falla had sent Debussy from Granada.

S.A. What a feeling for synthesis! That's how one can recognize genius!

F.P. Obviously it's genius.

S.A. Tell me, which of Manuel de Falla's works do you prefer?

F.P. The *Retablo* without doubt. I think it's a wonderful masterpiece. I don't know if I shall make myself fully understood, but I'd like to talk about it a bit from the technical point of view. Because of the form that's peculiar to it, neither cantata, oratorio or opera, the *Retablo* has always seemed to me to be a *musical object*, like those masterpieces by Renaissance goldsmiths where the most precious stones are set pell-mell, but with what genius, in a superb mount. The form of the *Retablo* is in fact odd. It is a series of short episodes linked by recitatives, the whole ending up with a long aria by Don Quixote. At first glance it may look loosely put together, but it's nothing of the kind, because a secret architecture presides over the working-out of the piece. Falla, in fact, didn't possess the sense of form so dominant in a Ravel or a Bartók. In this respect it's amusing to compare the bacchanale which ends *Daphnis et Chloé* and the finale of the *Sombrero de tres picos*. With Ravel the music advances superbly; with Falla it paws the ground in the same place all the time, which doesn't really matter at all because it's a Spanish dance.

S.A. Obviously a zapateado, in fact.

F.P. Look, for example, at Falla's *Fantasia bética* for piano—it's played very rarely. It's wonderfully written for the keyboard, but the reason it isn't played is because it constantly turns round on itself, while the pieces in Albéniz' *Iberia*, for example, soar from the piano to the back of the hall. Look, what is inspired in the *Retablo* is the feat of having translated musically, as Falla did, the part of the spokesman, that is, the little boy who introduces the show. Falla entrusted this part to a child's voice, or, if necessary, a very shrill soprano. You know the episode in Cervantes that gave Falla his idea. It's the one where Don Quixote stops for the night in a hostelry, a tavern, and after supper a puppet master puts on a show. It's the story of Melisendra rescued from the Moors by Roland, Charlemagne's nephew. A child announces what each scene is to show. At the end, when the Moors rush forward in pursuit of the fugitives, Don Quixote runs them through with his sword and breaks all the puppets. To tell the truth, a stage performance of this work is almost impossible because it was conceived for the Princesse de Polignac's drawing-room and doesn't adapt to a larger setting. So one must enjoy it in the concert hall, and there it's really first class. The orchestration is wonderful, and the important thing is that for the first time Falla incorporated the harpsichord into the modern orchestra. It was excellently played at the first performance in the Princesse de Polignac's house. Naturally, because it was Wanda Landowska who took the harpsichord part.

S.A. You couldn't wish for a better!

F.P. I'll ask you to believe it was very good. Wanda was killing about it, actually. She said: "At last, at last you won't treat me like a superannuated old dowager any more! All the

Manuel de Falla

composers here must write for me, because the harpsichord isn't a museum piece." That was how Falla came to promise to write her a harpsichord concerto. He did so, and later I wrote my *Concert champêtre* for Landowska. You can't imagine what those rehearsals of the *Retablo* at the Princesse de Polignac's were like. It was fascinating, because you discovered a new Falla, a new Spain. It was no longer the Andalusia of *El amor brujo* but Castille with its Escorial . . . It was astonishing, in fact, I must say that the more I hear the orchestration of the *Retablo* the more it fascinates me because I feel I'm rediscovering it each time, and that, don't you see, is the miracle of ORCH-EST-RAT-ION that's really *felt*. You can always write well, orchestrate well, but you don't always *feel* the orchestra. That's what's so astonishing about Falla and Ravel. With Ravel for example, *L'Enfant et les sortilèges* . . . It begins: the conductor raises his baton . . . and you say, ah yes, it's true . . . we're going to hear two wonderful oboes . . . but that's not it at all . . . suddenly your hope is surpassed and the concert hall smells of the country . . . that's the miracle . . . that's what's marrrvellous! So I say it, without being at all flowery, the *Retablo* smells of Castillian wine, the *queso manchego*, that thoroughbred Spanish cheese.

S.A. You're making my mouth water, I desperately want to get to know that cheese . . . But let's not talk of food, we'd never end. Let's come back to Falla, instead . . . We were talking of his harpsichord concerto.

F.P. It's a magnificent work, and this time one is very close to Saint John of the Cross. It's also a piece to be played at the Escorial. The Andante is very off-putting . . . it's an extraordinary piece. It's a sort of liturgical piece, very, very 'aston-n-n-ishing'.

S.A. This concerto is dedicated to Wanda Landowska, isn't it?

My Friends and Myself

F.P. Yes.

S.A. So I conclude as a result that she gave the first performance?

F.P. No, no, she didn't. She never played it.

S.A. Oh? Why?

F.P. It was the object of a semi-quarrel between Wanda and Falla. Falla worked very very slowly, and to begin with he'd sent the first part to Wanda who was waiting for it with impatience. She was delighted from the musical point of view but disappointed instrumentally. She wanted changes, and Falla, finding there were too many of them for his liking, refused to modify the thing. In the end it was Falla himself who played this work in Paris for the first time, round about the years 1927-1928, in the old Salle Pleyel in the Opéra district.

S.A. It's destroyed today. I wouldn't like to end this conversation without asking you if you've any knowledge of that posthumous manuscript they discovered among Falla's papers called *La Atlántida*? Could you talk to us about it?

F.P. Listen! Listen! *La Atlántida* is totally unknown for everyone. It makes no difference my being the friend of Halffter, and Roland-Manuel too, who's Falla's musicographer, we none of us know the work. Ernesto Halffter is Falla's favourite pupil; for years he's been completing Falla's manuscript, which some say is half-finished, others scarcely in draft form. Obviously I always distrust posthumous works, but Halffter has a profound respect for Falla, just as Falla admired Halffter enormously. The best we can do is wait for the first performance... We can't talk about it before.[1]

[1] A concert performance of *La Atlántida* was given in Barcelona on the 24th November, 1961. The first stage performance of Ernesto Halffter's completed version was given on the 16th April, 1962, at La Scala, Milan, and the score published the same year by Ricordi. Poulenc would have been able to get to know it, since he did not die until the January of 1963. [Translator.]

4

PAUL ÉLUARD

Stéphane Audel.
>Je suis né derrière une façade affreuse
>J'ai mangé j'ai ri j'ai rêvé j'ai eu honte
>J'ai vécu comme une ombre
>Et pourtant j'ai su chanter le soleil
>Le soleil entier celui qui respire
>Dans chaque poitrine et dans tous les yeux
>La goutte de candeur qui luit après les larmes.[1]

Those admirable lines define their author perfectly, the poet you're going to speak of today; your friend Paul Éluard. Will you talk about him? And let me once again ask you the ritual question: where and how did you meet Paul Éluard?

Francis Poulenc. I knew Paul Éluard in 1916. I was then seventeen and Paul was three or four years older. 1916 is an important year for the history of French art in every sphere: painting, music, sculpture, poetry... After two years of war that had plunged Paris into a sort of lethargy, people had ended up by getting used to that tragic state of affairs, if I dare say as much. During the 1914 war the civilian population only suffered small material hardships... So life in the arts

---

[1] I was born behind a frightful front / I've eaten laughed dreamed and been ashamed / I have lived like a shadow / And yet I've been able to hymn the sun / The whole sun that breathes / In every breast and every eye / The drop of purity that shines after tears. *Poésie et vérité*, Gallimard, 1942.

My Friends and Myself

had picked up and the avant-garde raised its head again. Of course, Apollinaire, Léger, Braque, Derain, Vlaminck were still in the army, but Apollinaire had been withdrawn to Paris after his serious wound, and the painters, having been recalled to camouflage centres near the capital, could frequently come to Paris. Blaise Cendrars, who'd lost an arm in the war, was finally demobilized. Valéry, Gide, Claudel, Proust, were too old to be soldiers. Everything began to mix together in the extraordinary melting-pot of Paris. Of course, there was the "Nouvelle Revue française" group, the "Apollinaire" group, the "Cendrars" group, the "Cocteau" group, but all the writers, when they went in the direction of the Luxembourg, were in the habit of stopping at a bookshop now, alas, vanished: Adrienne Monnier's at No. 7, rue de l'Odéon. If you pushed open the door of the Monnier bookshop between four and seven o'clock in the evening, most of the time you'd find there Léon-Paul Fargue, who was the presiding spirit of the place, Valéry Larbaud and James Joyce. They were the faithful followers, the regulars; and then frequently the most varied types of writer crossed the threshold: Valéry quite as often as Max Jacob, Paul Claudel as often as Apollinaire. I was introduced to Adrienne Monnier in 1915 by a friend who's dead now, Raymonde Linossier, to whose memory I dedicated my ballet *Les Animaux modèles*, and I became an intimate of the shop. Now, one afternoon in 1916 three young people I scarcely knew by name crossed the threshold of the shop: they were André Breton, Paul Éluard and Louis Aragon. If I remember rightly Breton was wearing the uniform of an army doctor, Aragon was too and I think Éluard was a soldier as well, but I don't recall exactly. Breton impressed me immediately with that leonine manner of his, the way he carried his head thrown back; Aragon, pink and fair haired, amused me enormously with his gift of the gab, his nerve, and his busybody side that made him go round inspecting the bookshop

Paul Éluard

down to the slightest detail. When he didn't like one of the books displayed—and Heaven knows there were plenty of them—he amused himself for a bit by turning back the covers. Paul Éluard listened in silence and watched, if I can describe it like this, with loving indolence. There was always love in everything Éluard did. Adrienne Monnier introduced us but I felt myself of very little account in front of those chaps who'd already published writings in the avant-garde magazines. None of them, what's more, was interested in music, in spite of Adrienne Monnier's kindly: "He's such a gifted boy!" As I told you just now, avant-garde magazines were beginning to spring up everywhere and it was round about this time that Breton, Aragon and Éluard founded the magazine *Littérature* which was the start of the Surrealist movement. Leafing through *Littérature* last autumn I was interested to see that some of Apollinaire's and Max Jacob's best poems appeared there for the first time and that it was in *Littérature* that Valéry's famous "Palmes" and "Cantiques des Colonnes" saw the light of day. After many shouts and peals of laughter from Aragon, violent declarations from Breton and a few firm and gentle replies from Éluard, the three nonconformists withdrew leaving me dazzled and dumbstruck! A few days after, in the same bookshop, I saw Éluard again, alone, returning a book she'd lent him to Adrienne Monnier. No one looked after books better than Paul Éluard. You'd lend him a book with a worn cover and he'd give it back to you carefully gummed up, ironed out, covered with transparent paper . . . and that for a book of no value at all! That's what explains Paul Éluard's love of books, a love he carried to extremes all his life. The first time I saw that brilliant trio I was a bit nonplussed. At close quarters with Éluard I saw him better. On his own he spoke this time with gentle eloquence. I lost my shyness, asked him many a question, and, without realizing it, gave him my friendship that day. Later on I came to love

My Friends and Myself

Paul and he returned it to me with interest, with a real brotherly love. Adrienne Monnier, with good reason, liked to hear writers read their works aloud. "It always reveals something to you that you hadn't suspected when you read the book yourself," she used to say. That's the truth.

S.A. Absolutely!

F.P. And so an old record of Apollinaire or of Éluard teaches us a lot more about their poetic secrets than the digressions of their commentators.

S.A. Certainly.

F.P. What a lot of fascinating readings took place at Adrienne Monnier's! I heard Gide read *Le Retour de l'Enfant Prodigue*, Valéry read *Le Cimetière marin* and *La Jeune Parque*, and Claudel *L'Ours et la lune* . . . That's not a bad memory to have!

S.A. It's remarkable.

F.P. Of course, for a musician the ear is often a safer guide than the eye in poetry. So at Adrienne Monnier's request, and without further urging, Éluard, in that warm voice of his, read a few poems he took out of his brief-case, gentle and passionate by turns, muffled and metallic. At that precise moment I didn't realize it at all, but unknown to me Éluard had just settled a large part of my fate as a composer.

S.A. Yes, I can believe that. Since you knew your friend Éluard so young and so closely immediately, how did it come about that you waited until 1935 before writing your first songs to his poems?

F.P. It's odd indeed, but to tell you the truth I think I didn't believe myself capable of setting Éluard to music. Incidentally, I'd point out to you that if, in 1918, I wrote *Le Bestiaire* at the age of nineteen, until 1931 I'd written very few songs.

S.A. You've made up for it since, thank God! When Breton,

Paul Éluard

Aragon, Éluard, Dali and Max Ernst founded the Surrealist group, did you join with them?

F.P. No, I never belonged directly to the Surrealist group because there was no room there for a musician. Anyway, they all detested music. For Breton, for example, music had no meaning, it was useless and cumbersome. At the end of his life Éluard became more accessible to it, and Aragon listens to it willingly, but without any great pleasure. Yet if I didn't belong to the Surrealist group I had many friends apart from Breton, Aragon and Éluard. I was very fond of René Crevel and Desnos. I sometimes went and met the group at the Cintra bar, in the passage de l'Opéra, which no longer exists now, and which Aragon has described so wonderfully in *Anicet ou le Panorama*.

S.A. You've always been independent, it's a part of your nature. But let's get back to Paul Éluard, shall we? Didn't he inspire your early choral works and, later, much more important works?

F.P. Yes, yes, of course. Once I'd discovered the secret of Éluard's prosody I never stopped setting him to music. For a very long time I didn't know how to set about it . . . but once I'd found the key . . . the cipher . . . I understood. Then I happened to say quite often to Paul Éluard: "Poor Paul, I'm going to slaughter you a little bit more . . ." "I'm glad of it," he'd say politely, "but do it quickly, I'm so impatient to hear you . . ." His friendship adapted itself to all my requests. For example, a title which is good for a book isn't necessarily a good one for a group of songs. When I set poems taken from *Les Yeux fertiles*, I said to Éluard: "Listen, it's very visual, it works when the poems appear alongside engravings, illustrations by Picasso, but it's not suitable for music. Imagine someone asking what you're going to sing. *Les Yeux fertiles*? It's not very . . ." So then Paul, who was always wonderfully good to me, sent me several titles, and the one I chose for a song cycle of mine that's quite well known was *Tel jour, telle nuit*. If I've written many songs to Éluard poems I think I've written even more choral works to them. My first *a cappella* piece was composed to five poems by Éluard and two by Apollinaire. It's called *Sept chansons*. I've also written a little cantata, *Soir de neige*, and, especially, one of my major works, *Figure humaine*, for double *a cappella* chorus, composed during the Occupation to the famous poems in the volume *Poésie et vérité*. This is the volume that includes *Liberté*. The work is, unfortunately, very difficult, and so it's hardly ever sung.

S.A. I'd like you now, Francis, in the light of your experience as artist and collaborator, to talk to us about Éluard as a man and as a poet.

F.P. Listen, it's not easy to depict Paul Éluard, you know. If, in our early conversations, I was able to sketch Erik Satie, Max Jacob and Manuel de Falla easily, here the case is quite different. At first glance Éluard was a man like any other, and nothing in his manner drew him particularly to your attention. You had to know him well to sense the poet in him. He didn't wear a plaid shawl on his shoulders like Mallarmé, he didn't display the Bohemian manner of a Verlaine or a Rimbaud, he didn't flaunt Théophile Gautier's red waistcoat, nor even the heavy, shapeless outline so characteristic of Apollinaire. Personally, I always thought Éluard very handsome, for his features were arranged in noble lines. But he was quietly handsome. Note that an inner fire smouldered under that apparent calm. I've seen him in terrible rages, but also in far more wonderful moments of gentleness when his warm and caressing voice literally cast a spell on you. It was wonderful to hear him read Baudelaire and his own poems. There was no more faithful, more watchful friend than Éluard. People who

Paul Éluard

liked him could never inconvenience him. An example: looking for a title for my ballet on La Fontaine fables and not being able to find it, I asked Éluard, who immediately sent me a letter suggesting *Les Animaux modèles*, which I instantly took possession of for myself. You wouldn't realize, Stéphane, how terrible a gap Éluard's death left me with! I didn't know Apollinaire well, so I can say without heresy that Éluard was my favourite poet!

S.A. Yes, I believe it. Actually I was present when Éluard died and I saw your feeling was deep and real. The general opinion is that your work, what you created to Éluard's poems, is outstanding, but that your most famous group is unquestionably *Tel jour, telle nuit*.

F.P. Certainly.

S.A. It's the best known, but I'll admit I've a special weakness for the song cycle *La Fraîcheur et le feu*. Did you write it during Éluard's lifetime, Francis?

F.P. Yes, yes, yes. I composed *La Fraîcheur et le feu* in . . . let's see . . . wait a bit . . . in 1950, that's two years before Paul's death. I'm glad you like that song cycle because it hardly ever gets sung, and if I've a little weakness for it, then it's perhaps because it's got a very special form. In fact it consists of seven sections, not seven songs. Basically it was the very cut of the poem that led me to write a big song in seven sections rather than a series of songs. And that's what's very special, what I like in *La Fraîcheur et le feu*.

S.A. Now, Francis, let's broach, if you will, another aspect and not one of the least important of the poet. Let's not talk about groupings or commitment where he's concerned, I don't much like words of that nature . . .

F.P. Neither do I, you know . . . He was committed to poetry alone anyway.

My Friends and Myself

S.A. Yes, that was his commitment.

F.P. Exactly.

S.A. He was a poet, in fact, who wrote:

> Le seul rêve des innocents
> Un seul murmure, un seul matin
> Et les saisons à l'unisson
> Colorant de neige et de feu
> Une foule enfin réunie . . .[1]

The man who wrote the immortal stanzas of *Liberté* naturally held a well-defined intellectual viewpoint . . . He combined the religion of justice, the religion of freedom, with love of man.

F.P. You might say, since love was all with Éluard, that it was through love of humanity and peace that he joined a political party that seemed to him destined to bring the happiness he wished for men. Some are free to regret this commitment, even outside of political matters, but we should bear in mind that this commitment made Éluard lose none of his deep qualities, and that he at least, by contrast with many others, never sank into facile poetic tub-thumping. Do you understand? He didn't turn into a Déroulède of the Communist party, he always remained a wonderful poet.[2]

S.A. He remained honest and untouched, and you're perfectly right to say that all was love with him. I don't think I'm giving way to a temptation of unworthy curiosity in

---

[1] The single dream of the innocent / A single whisper, a single morning / And the seasons in unison / Colouring with snow and fire / A crowd now gathered together . . . *Pentes inférieures*, Gallimard.

[2] A discreet reference to the contortions of certain writers, alive and much honoured today, who joined the French Communist Party. Poulenc tactfully hedges his bet by mentioning Paul Déroulède, a byword for Right-wing demagogy. [Translator.]

Paul Éluard

asking you to tell us about the women Éluard loved, the poems they inspired in him?

F.P. Éluard married three times and basically each of his wives corresponded very closely to his evolution as man and poet. The first, "Gala", a Jewess, very clever, was his wife during the Surrealist period. She's since become Salvador Dali's wife. I've never been very close with Gala . . . but she told my fortune from cards wonderfully ! ! !

S.A. She knew how to tell fortunes?

F.P. Wonderrrfully !

S.A. She predicted your future?

F.P. Well, not the whole of my future, but once, at a session with the cards, she was extraordinary. The second : "Nouche", was the wonderful inspiration of Éluard's great poetic period. She was an exquisite creature, charming. You can check this from countless photos, many of them in Éluard's slim volumes. Picasso also drew and painted her many times. To her beauty and elegance the adorable Nouche joined all the qualities of a perfect housewife. Éluard never had to worry about anything during the hard Occupation years, and when she died suddenly of a burst blood-vessel it was a dreadful sorrow for Éluard and a real dismay to us all. We didn't know what was to become of him. Fortunately his daughter, Gala and Éluard's daughter that is, Picasso, and René Char, were really unrivalled friends to him. They didn't abandon him, they didn't leave him; but he spent excruciating months, excruciating years, and after all this moral and physical decay, Éluard met the woman who became his third wife, Dominique. Dominique is a strong woman as the Bible says; she was excellent during his last years. Then Éluard picked up courage again and a taste for life. Happiness returned to his home and his lyricism rediscovered its warmth.

5

ARTHUR HONEGGER

Stéphane Audel. I'd like you to talk to me today, Francis about one of the friends of your youth: Arthur Honegger. When did you meet him for the first time?

Francis Poulenc. I met Arthur Honegger . . . I think I can tell you exactly . . . in the Spring of 1917. At that time I was a piano student of Ricardo Viñes, and Viñes had literally adopted me as a sort of favourite pupil. I didn't deserve the favour perhaps, but he carted me about everywhere with him, and one day he said to me: "You must meet Jane Bathori." Naturally I much admired Jane Bathori, that great singer who was the first to perform all of Debussy's songs, Ravel's . . . and then, in the spring of 1917, I began to go regularly on Sundays to her house where you could make music with professionals, artists. It was absolutely delightful, and that was how I heard, before everyone else, Debussy's Sonata for harp, flute and viola, which was more or less sight-read from the manuscript. I must tell you that André Caplet, an excellent musician and great friend of Debussy, was also a close friend of Jane Bathori, and through him we usually got music by Debussy or Ravel hot off the press and read it enthusiastically at sight. One day he decided we should sight-read Ravel's three wonderful *a cappella* songs. We shared the task out between us. Naturally, Bathori and a few pupils took the soprano and mezzo parts, and the bass and baritone parts were given to my teacher

Arthur Honegger

Charles Koechlin, with that beard of his like a river god's, Honegger, me, and so on. That was the first time I'd seen Honegger, and while we were singing those Ravel songs I made mistakes once or twice. Arthur Honegger turned round and said to me: "Ear training . . . young man?" for you mustn't forget that Arthur was seven years older than me. At that time I was eighteen and he was twenty-five, which obviously meant I should defer to him when it came to the pinch. I was very intimidated, and perhaps it was because of that first contact that Honegger scared me for a very long time.

S.A. It could very well be . . . yes.

F.P. Yes of course. Although we were young men together, he was seven years older; remember, too, that Milhaud was also seven years older than me.

S.A. But I seem to recall Milhaud wasn't yet in Paris at that time.

F.P. No, he was still in Brazil. I've never been over-awed by Milhaud for an instant, because he had a very different manner. Arthur, with that handsome, serious face of his, had intimidated me. Also among the singers in that little choir was Andrée Vaurabourg, who later became Madame Honegger. In short, my first contact with Arthur was one that certainly didn't foreshadow closer acquaintanceship, Les Six . . . nothing at all of that! We were simply two musicians, one of them already vaguely experienced, the other a complete beginner, who happened to meet at Jane Bathori's . . . you know that later on Jane Bathori took over the management of the Théâtre du Vieux Colombier. You remember that when Copeau left for America, Jane Bathori had the idea of organizing some concerts, and that's how Arthur became not only a comrade but a great friend.

S.A. It seems to me that at the meetings of Les Six and the

meetings you had among yourselves, you used to meet Arthur Honegger less often than the others. Why?

F.P. That's not quite correct. When Henri Collet, the critic of *Comoedia*, christened us "the Group of the Six", on the model of the five Russians, with that label on our backs we all belonged to the same stable. Even so, I used to see a lot of Honegger, because every week we held what we called the "Saturday Dinner". In the beginning we'd meet at Darius Milhaud's. He lived next to the rue Chaptal. We drank cocktails there (the years after the 1914 war were the cocktail period), and we met Jean Cocteau, Jean Hugo, Auric, Fauconnet and Radiguet. We'd also meet at Germaine Tailleferre's, then we'd go off to dine in a Montmartre restaurant ... We used to see Arthur, every Saturday, very regularly, and as a result we were constantly in touch. What might make you think I saw less of Arthur was the fact that it was very difficult to get him at home. It was already very difficult when he lived in the rue Duperré, but afterwards it became harder still when he lived on the boulevard de Clichy, because Arthur never answered the telephone ... when the door-bell rang he didn't open up; when you wrote to him he didn't reply. It wasn't that I didn't want to be close to Arthur, but I telephoned Milhaud nearly every day, I rang Auric nearly every day too, so that we often saw each other between Saturdays. My friendship with Arthur wasn't what my friendship with Milhaud and Auric was. The paradoxical thing about it is that my great intimacy with Honegger only occurred during the last two years of his life, because he was ill. When he was ill he liked you to come and see him and keep him company...

S.A. You're jumping ahead a bit there, Francis ...

F.P. Yes, I'm anticipating rather, but it's only to show you the general curve of our friendship. The point of departure and the arrival.

Arthur Honegger

S.A. Let's go back a bit, if you will, because there's a question I want to ask you, one I've often asked myself. Diaghilev produced *Les Biches* at Monte Carlo in 1924, the very year when Honegger's *Le Roi David* was given in oratorio form in Paris. I'd like to know what you each thought of the other's music at that time. Honegger of yours and you of Honegger's.

F.P. I must tell you, to speak frankly, that Arthur found my music too light and I found his too heavy! Naturally, in the end we judged each other quite differently. But we were then, in fact, travelling divergent ways. We admired each other greatly, but we didn't like each other's music until the end of Arthur's life.

S.A. I'd like to ask you too why Diaghilev, who commissioned ballets from Stravinsky, Prokofiev, Darius Milhaud, Georges Auric, Erik Satie, and from you—since he produced *Les Biches*—why he never called on Honegger's talent?

F.P. Well, yes, that's a question I've asked myself several times, but, you know, if Diaghilev never commissioned anything from Honegger, that's no reason to construe it as an adverse judgement on his part. Diaghilev admired Honegger, he admired Roussel, he admired Léger, but he never commissioned anything either from Roussel or Léger. He needed a sort of familiarity with music, with painting, and he didn't find it with Honegger. There's one thing I can tell you: Diaghilev was a very jealous man, *terribly* jealous, and the sole fact that Arthur worked for the dancer Ida Rubinstein was enough for Diaghilev not to commission anything from him... Anyway, in another direction, Madame Rubinstein ignored me all her life! She never asked me for anything.

S.A. Which of Honegger's works do you admire most?

F.P. What do I admire above all?... I admire lots of things ... The one I admire above all is *Antigone*!

My Friends and Myself

S.A. It's very odd you should tell me that, because Honegger himself—in Lausanne, during the recording of William Aguet's *Saint François d'Assise*, for which he wrote the music—said to me in a friendly way, in a corner of the studio: "Yes, people are always talking about *Jeanne au bûcher* and *Le Roi David*. Well, I'll tell you myself that I prefer *Antigone* of all my music!" You see, he thought like you.

F.P. Yes. It's a rare and wonderful work, and he put the best of himself into it. I'll tell you: what I've sometimes criticized Honegger's music for isn't due to him, it's due to his collaborators. Yes. And perhaps what I like least in *La Danse des morts* is its conventional side, revolutionary dances and all that. That's not his fault, it's Claudel's.

S.A. Yet you'll admit that the encounter between Claudel and Honegger brought magnificent results!

F.P. Naturally, but I think he wasn't in luck with Claudel. Darius Milhaud had the best Claudel, because I think that Claudel's last period . . . well, let's face things squarely, let's speak clearly: *Jeanne au bûcher* owed its success to Honegger, but not to Claudel!

S.A. And what are your favourites among the symphonic works?

F.P. Oh, so far as the symphonic works are concerned I'm like many people, as to be expected: the Symphony for strings and trumpet, and the Fifth, the Symphony 'di tre re', which really has something very rare about it. I very much like the Fourth Symphony he wrote for Paul Sacher, for the Basle Chamber Orchestra. I must admit it's a charming symphony, with, let's say it, Arthur's Swiss affinities, the feeling of freshness, the mountains, pure air, edelweiss. I like that symphony a lot, I'd say.

S.A. Don't you find, Francis, that Honegger's chamber music is very unjustly neglected at the moment?

Arthur Honegger

F.P. I'm astonished that string groups never play Honegger's quartets. One of Arthur's best things, one of the works most full of musical wit, is his first quartet. And the third has perfect balance. But you get oddities like that: all composers have their eclipse, and suddenly a quartet comes into the picture. A Hungarian quartet will play Honegger's Third and immediately Honegger's Third will be played by all other quartets throughout the whole world.

S.A. The success of Le Roi David and Jeanne au bûcher have harmed the rest of Honegger's work.

F.P. Arthur was very irritated by that success. He always said: "That's all you ever hear." I don't say Le Roi David doesn't come off, far from it. But if you put Antigone and Le Roi David in the scales . . . it's Antigone that tips them!

S.A. Since we're talking of Le Roi David, I'd like to ask you something that concerns you directly. Why have you never attempted oratorio as a means of musical expression?

F.P. The reason is what you'd expect. Arthur wrote oratorios because he was a Protestant whereas I've written masses, motets, a Gloria, a Stabat Mater and an Office de la semaine sainte, because I'm a Catholic. It's simply a matter of religious upbringing. I set prayer to music and he set religious history. It's quite different.

S.A. That's what I thought and you've just confirmed it for me. Honegger had a very distinguished career, one of early brilliance, because he knew success in his youth . . .

F.P. That's true.

S.A. And so I'm surprised to find thoughts like these from his pen: "Your contemporaries always need someone to sell them soap or noodles, they've no need whatever of new music," or again: "The young composer is a man who persists in creating a product that no one wants to consume!" What pessimism! What disillusionment!

My Friends and Myself

F.P. I think Arthur had a sort of presentiment of the shortness of his life, his illness and approaching death. And I'm sure of it, because one day, being ill myself, I said to him: "You with your wonderful health!" and he replied sadly:
Ah, we don't know who'll die first!" I think at the end, especially, he had no illusions about his illness, and in fact I've a very upsetting memory in that respect. One day I'd been to play to him an extract from Le Dialogue des Carmélites (it was Arthur who'd asked me to), and after hearing it he said to me: "Listen, I've a notebook—a music exercisebook—I planned to write something in, it's the same as the one you've always used (for, in fact, we both of us used the same sort of notebooks), I'd like you to keep it and write something in it, because I shall write no more music myself." I can tell you, I keep it as a relic, but I'm incapable of writing in that notebook. That tone of pessimism, that tone of pain had made him all the more human. I don't know whether you remember that one day, in my house, I showed you one of the last letters I received from Arthur. It's a remarkable letter, with a little too much praise of me in it. It will define exactly, as a conclusion to our talk, the terms we were on with Arthur at the time of his death. A very great tenderness, indeed, for tenderness is the word we should use, and I must say it was during the last three years of his life that we really understood one another, that we talked about everything.

S.A. That letter was sent to you by Arthur Honegger on the 10th May, 1954. He was then in Basle with his friends the Sachers, who showed him admirable devotion to the end. Here it is:

My dear Francis,
I've just received a copy of your 'Conversations'.[1]

[1] The reference is to the conversations organized with Poulenc by Claude Rostand on the French radio and published by Julliard as Entretiens avec Claude Rostand in 1954. [Translator.]

Arthur Honegger

I read them on the spot. I can tell you that reading them has brought me extraordinarily close to you. It's increased the affection I have for you as a loyal friend and enlarged the admiration I have for you as a musician, a man who is a natural creator of music, a difference which distinguishes you so greatly from so many others. In the thick of the methods, systems, shibboleths that impotent people have tried to impose, you have remained yourself with that rare courage that demands respect. We have, I think, very different temperaments, but I think I have this in common with you, a love of music rather than a love of success. We express ourselves similarly on opposing points. You declare your love for Satie and your lack of understanding of Fauré. I myself began by regarding Fauré as an elegant drawing-room composer and now he is one of my greatest enthusiasms, while I look on Satie as having an excessively precise mind but bereft of all creative power. Do what I say, above all don't do what I do! We both of us love the energy of Strauss, we both prefer a successful *Louise* by Charpentier to a lamentable flop such as Dukas' *Ariane et Barbe-bleue*. You don't subscribe yourself only in the name of Berlioz alone, in whom people admire everything they detest in Beethoven, Wagner or Schumann. You understand the silliness of trampling on Wagner in 1954; it's like asking the Paris Council to tear up the Eiffel Tower, one of its most flourishing attractions; but you hope never to hear *Die Meistersinger* again, whereas it's something I hope will live on. You don't like van Gogh, for whom I'd exchange the whole of Toulouse-Lautrec, van Gogh whom I admire as you do El Greco. All these divergences, far from separating us, seem on the contrary to bring us together. Isn't variety the finest thing in life and in art? Don't think me too presumptuous if I put myself beside you to say: 'We are two civilized men!'

Je t'embrasse en fraternelle affection.
Arthur Honegger.[1]

[1] This letter, quoted in *Francis Poulenc, Correspondence, 1915–1963*, Editions du Seuil, 1967, also has a postscript sending good wishes from personal friends. [Translator.]

6

SERGE PROKOFIEV

Stéphane Audel. In 1921, at the Théâtre Sarah Bernhardt, the Russian Ballet performed Serge Prokofiev's *Chout*. Did you already know Prokofiev at the time of *Chout's* first performance, Francis?

Francis Poulenc. It was precisely at that time that I did know him. I knew him through the medium of Diaghilev, in the atmosphere of the Russian Ballet. The first time I saw him was at a lunch to which Diaghilev had invited me in the Hôtel Continental. Diaghilev was in Paris at that time for a season, the season in fact when they did *Chout* for the first time. I remember that Prokofiev's collaborators were at that lunch, too. There was the Larionov-Gontcharova pair who'd designed the scenery for *Chout*. There was Leonide Massine who'd done the choreography. I was very impressed by that first contact with Prokofiev, because it was quite different from the first contact you were likely to have with Stravinsky. With Stravinsky one was, and always has been, dazzled by superior powers of argument, by points of view sometimes paradoxical but always brilliant and always exact. With Prokofiev, on the other hand, all was silence. I don't think I've remembered four sentences, four words, from Prokofiev at that lunch.

S.A. Very odd.

F.P. He was a quiet man. Besides that, I was very young;

Serge Prokofiev

he knew nothing about me, there was perhaps a little disdain in his attitude, at any rate there was nothing to make you foresee we were going to become very good friends.

S.A. I think, in fact, that of all the musicians Prokofiev met while staying in Paris and in France, you're the only one he became friendly with. But since this friendship didn't spring from your first meeting, how did it show itself?

F.P. My friendship with Prokofiev was based on two things. First, we each of us had a liking for the piano—I played a lot with him, I helped him practise his concertos—and then something else that has nothing to do with music: a liking for bridge. At that time I played bridge very well, I can say it all the more now without false modesty, since I play very badly these days. But at that time I played a lot, and Prokofiev was very keen on bridge. Last summer, when I was sorting out a big bundle of correspondence from musicians, poets, painters, at my home in the country, and came across some from Prokofiev, I realized there wasn't a single letter, I think, in which bridge wasn't referred to. Here, for example, is what he wrote me from Ciboure in September, 1931:

> Dear Francis,
> Our great bridge tournament will take place towards the end of October and I hope it'll be very musical so far as the players are concerned: in the meantime, I'm practising with Thibaud and Chaliapin. I've had a card from Iceland, from Alekhin, the chess champion, who asks me when the bridge tournament is fixed for, too.

In another letter, still in the same year, in October, 1931, he says to me:

> Dear Francis,
> I shall be very happy to see you at the end of November so as to be able to play in the bridge tournament. By the way, if

My Friends and Myself

your business affairs [I'd lost a lot of money at the time] aren't going on very well, you ought to take part in the bridge competition organized by *Judge*, a New York weekly, which is offering 25,000 dollars as a prize; that's not like Mrs Coolidge's modest 1,000 [she'd given us commissions at the time of 1,000 dollars apiece]. The competition consists of ten problems to solve, and everyone can take part. Think about it carefully.

S.A. How quaint!

F.P. Isn't it? In each letter, I could have chosen a third extract, it's nothing but bridge . . . I ought to add that, especially in 1931 and 1932, we used to meet nearly every week at Prokofiev's in the evening, with Jacques Février—he was an excellent bridge player—Alekhin, whom Prokofiev speaks of in his letter—and a Russian lady who played extremely well. Usually we spent our evenings playing. Music was an extra. If I arrived early, we'd have a cold dinner and play music for four hands . . . There . . . That's the point where my friendship with Serge crystallized.

S.A. But I imagine all the same that Prokofiev must have been interested in many other things apart from bridge? Can you tell us, for example, if on the literary side he was curious about French writers, as it was only natural for him to be interested in Russian ones? For example, what had he read of Marcel Proust?

F.P. I'll tell you. Prokofiev spoke French admirably, he wrote French very well. On reading his letters again, from the point of view of style and spelling, I cannot think of him as a Russian.

S.A. He had no difficulty in reading poetry as a result?

F.P. Poetry? I don't think French poetry moved him, I don't think Rimbaud . . .

S.A. And Verlaine? Max Jacob?

Serge Prokofiev

F.P. He wasn't interested in it . . . He wasn't interested in Gide, because I think Gide had too logical, too Cartesian a mind for a Russian. He was more interested in Proust, obviously, but I think that what interested him above all else was life and the history of religions. In fact his opera *The Fiery Angel*—an excellent opera—well represents this interest in religion.

S.A. He was like Mussorgsky, who based *Khovanshchina* on a religious question involving the old believers.

F.P. Yes, it's the same thing. That's more or less what he did with *The Fiery Angel*. Look, he wasn't completely uninterested in Balzac, for example, whom he could have understood wonderfully. No, no, no, he wasn't a literary man; he was a musician above all. Ravel didn't read much, but Ravel had poetic interests. I think I knew Prokofiev well enough to be able to state that, because he never talked to me about poets, and yet he was aware that I knew them all. No, music it was, really, and, if I dare say so, HIS MUSIC!

S.A. I understand. Now may I speak of a personal memory? I apologize, but it can be justified. In 1942, in Rio de Janeiro, Colonel de Basil, who managed a ballet company—and for that reason had bought back all of Diaghilev's scenery—was putting on Prokofiev's *The Prodigal Son* over there, in Georges Rouault's setting. The Colonel told me in confidence that not only did Prokofiev not approve of that production but he actively disliked it. Which leads me to ask you whether, following your example, like that of many composers like Stravinsky, Georges Auric, Henri Sauguet, whether Prokofiev appreciated, whether he liked painting?

F.P. No. And it's correct—quite correct—that Prokofiev loathed Rouault's scenery. He would have liked something more Russian for *The Prodigal Son* . . . you understand . . . he preferred Gontcharova and Larianov who'd done *Chout*. And

My Friends and Myself

that side... how shall I say? That Palestinian side to Rouault's scenery, perhaps rather a bit in the vein of "twilight on the Bosphorus". That scenery with its ochres and yellows and that moon up in the sky ... He didn't like it. So far as painting was concerned he did like Picasso's, of course. But that very fine portrait of him that Matisse painted, for example. We were all living together—and consequently it was quite natural that Matisse should do his portrait, as Picasso did mine—well, I think he was very pleased with that portrait and he thought it a good one. But I don't think he had any great liking for Matisse's style and painting. I repeat once more: music, HIS MUSIC.

S.A. And in the musical field, was he up to date with contemporary innovations? I'm thinking of Schoenberg, Webern, Alban Berg. He can't have ignored the existence of the Viennese school even so.

F.P. No, no, no. Naturally he knew that type of music, he knew all types. He was curious about them, but he only threw them a quick glance. All that went to make up the Viennese school at that time had no connection whatever with what he was doing. He was curious about it but not a bit ...

S.A. It didn't interest him?

F.P. He was more curious than interested, that's it, do you understand, that's what I mean. For example, *Wozzeck*, which, with *Pelléas et Mélisande*, is perhaps "the" masterpiece in opera this century, well, he certainly heard *Wozzeck*.

S.A. I was going to ask you ...

F.P. *Wozzeck* was first produced in 1925, to be precise. At that moment Prokofiev was doing a concert tour in Germany.

S.A. So he can't have been unaware of *Wozzeck*.

F.P. He listened to *Wozzeck*, he certainly saw it. *Wozzeck*

Serge Prokofiev

interested him but didn't affect him . . . He was curious about it because you can't if you're a musician like Prokofiev, you can't *not* be interested in the technical side . . . that extraordinary orchestral technique . . . But in fact, what interested him most was Stravinsky. Prokofiev was pre-eminently tonal and the "Great Igor's" music at that time, despite his harmonic daring, was still extremely tonal; as a result, basically, they both had something of the same language, although their music stands at opposite poles . . .

S.A. And what did Serge Prokofiev think of Francis Poulenc's music?

F.P. He thought badly of it, badly, but I didn't mind. Badly, I say, round about 1923. After that things changed. There's something that touched me. One day when I was in the street a Russian lady came up to me, a lady who'd aged considerably at that time (it was the lady who used to play bridge with us and Alekhin and Jacques Février). I spoke to her about Prokofiev who was then in Russia, and she confided in me that he said to her one day: "Well, you know, I was mistaken, Poulenc is a real musician" . . . so that consoled me, if ever I'd been hurt, that is. No, no, no, our relations boiled down to bridge, the piano and friendship. For example, he came to spend a weekend in the country at Noizay, (it was in June, 1932, before he left for America), and I remember his last weekend in my house. He'd brought a huge tin of caviar. Sauguet was there, so was Auric. We were all musicians, and of course it's a moving memory for me because they were all happy relationships, you understand.

S.A. Your chambermaid at Noizay talked to me about that gathering. She said: "I've never understood how people could like something that's so expensive and yet so nasty!"

F.P. She didn't like caviar?

S.A. She didn't like caviar.

My Friends and Myself

F.P. And it was a big tin, God knows. There must have been as much for the kitchen as there was for the guests' table!

S.A. Let's talk now about the pianist . . . because, independently of his career as a composer, Prokofiev made virtuoso appearances in Europe, America and Russia. Since you were familiar with his perfect technique as a pianist, how would you describe his playing?

F.P. Ah! . . . Prokofiev's playing!!! It was marrrvellous! I worshipped Prokofiev's playing. It was rather like Alfredo Casella's . . . He played on a level with the keyboard, with an extraordinary sureness of wrist, a marvellous staccato. He rarely attacked from on high; he wasn't at all the sort of pianist who throws himself from the fifth floor to produce the sound. He had a nervous power like steel, so that on a level with the keys he was capable of producing sonority of fantastic strength and intensity, and in addition—I recommend this to all players of Prokofiev's music—the tempo never, never varied. I had the honour of rehearsing all his concertos before his departure for America; I even rehearsed the first, which is never played, though it's very attractive and Richter has recorded it. I rehearsed his second concerto, of course, the third and the fifth. We rehearsed in the Salle Gaveau. It was June, we began . . . in shirtsleeves . . . afterwards, we took our shirts off . . . and in the end we were bare-chested . . . as if we were in Deauville. Prokofiev's rhythm was relentless, and sometimes, in the Fifth Concerto, when a very difficult passage cropped up, I'd say to Serge: "That's the orchestra, I'm doing what I can." He'd say to me: "Never mind, don't alter the tempo . . ."

S.A. Tempo . . . always Tempo . . .

F.P. That hammer-like tempo . . . hammer-like, unchanging. By the way, there's a very moving gramophone record of the Third Piano Concerto made by Prokofiev. It was re-issued in

Serge Prokofiev

the *Gravures illustres* series of famous recordings. I had the honour of presenting it, and I wrote: "It was a *re-lent-less* tempo."

S.A. Let's come back to the composer. Claude Manuel declares that "sometimes criticized as a revolutionary, sometimes as a neo-classic, Prokofiev was able to blend the traditional forms of Romantic diction with contemporary language in a style which is completely personal to him". What do you think of that definition?

F.P. To define Prokofiev's style . . . Stravinsky is a formidable innovator and Prokofiev isn't an innovator, but what does it matter? Schubert's not an innovator, either . . . Music wouldn't have changed if Schubert hadn't existed . . . do you understand? You can be a great musician and still not be an innovator . . . Yet you can be influenced by Prokofiev . . . I have myself, in certain little areas . . . But you can't say he was someone who made innovations like Debussy, like Schoenberg or Webern . . .

S.A. He wasn't a leader . . .

F.P. No. He was an excellent composer but he wasn't an innovator.

S.A. And he left a large body of work: it includes a hundred and thirty-eight opus numbers . . . However, it's not known in its entirety in western Europe. After his return to Russia in 1933 the composer wrote many works, which—putting on one side the scores for Eisenstein's films and the concertos that the virtuosos of his country have, if I may say so, exported—were never played in our part of the world. Let's not talk of his opera, *The Story of a Real Man*, which was violently attacked and brought about a momentary disgrace . . . Apart from his ballet *Romeo and Juliet* we know, through records and the radio, his opera *War and Peace* based on Tolstoy's novel. Do you know the score, Francis?

My Friends and Myself

F.P. Yes, I do.

S.A. There are some magnificent things in it, aren't there?

F.P. Yes, there are. But I've never seen the opera . . . Reading a score or hearing extracts from it doesn't give you the whole picture . . . you have to see the opera on the stage . . . For Prokofiev, it's an affecting score. Now, emotion isn't Prokofiev's dominating quality.

S.A. Certainly not.

F.P. But with this opera, in fact, you have something extraordinarily moving. Having said that, I think, without political prejudice, that Prokofiev's Russian work is much less fine, as opposed to the opinion of Russian writers on music that what he wrote in the West is less good.

S.A. Certainly. However, there were certain rules that had to be observed over there . . .

F.P. I'm not talking politics, but it's clear that certain works like the Sixth Symphony, the Seventh Symphony, don't possess much interest beside the rest. The Fifth is wonderful . . .

S.A. This gives me the opportunity of asking you a question that springs to mind: which of Prokofiev's works do you prefer?

F.P. Oh, there are . . . I can't tell you . . . because there are so many I like . . . I think that *The Fiery Angel* is obviously one of the peaks . . . *The Prodigal Son* is wonderful . . . the piano concertos, the violin concertos, are wonderful . . . I like the Second Symphony very much, the one where there's such a huge number of double-basses because it's a symphony dedicated to Koussevitzky, who was a double-bass player himself. I think the Fifth Symphony is superb . . . The Seventh Piano Sonata is always being played. It's not, perhaps, the finest, although the Andante is irresistible. The Sixth is very lovely. I don't understand why it's played so little . . . you know,

Serge Prokofiev

that's how it is . . . At the moment it doesn't get played, and since pianists are like Panurge's sheep, the day a great virtuoso plays it all the other pianists will play it. By contrast, I don't like the later sonatas. I don't like the Ninth. It seems to me like genuine Prokofiev . . . Still . . .

S.A. There are some superb things in the music he wrote for Eisenstein's films . . .

F.P. Ah yes, superb.

S.A. Which ones?

F.P. First, *Lieutenant Kizhe*.[1]

S.A. There's also *Ivan the Terrible*, and then *Alexander Nevsky*, especially . . . the Alexander Nevsky cantata . . .

F.P. It's magnificent, excellent . . . Prokofiev is a very great musician and I must say I retain an admiration for him that's loyal still, in spite of my interest in music he didn't like himself.

S.A. When did you see Prokofiev for the last time, Francis?

F.P. I saw him for the last time a few days after that famous weekend in 1932, which must have been round about the 5th or 6th June. We went on working together for about another week . . . There's a spot in Paris that's very moving for me. It's a bus-stop in the rue la Boétie, exactly at the corner of the faubourg Saint-Honoré, near the church of Saint-Philippe-du-Roule . . .

S.A. Yes, yes, I can see it very clearly.

F.P. We were coming out of the Salle Gaveau where we'd just been rehearsing. Serge got into the bus and said to me: "A bientôt". He waved to me with his hand. I shouted out: "Write to me . . ." And I never received anything . . . He went

[1] This film, after Tynyanov's novel, was in fact made not by Eisenstein but by Isaac Feinzimmer. It is also known as *The Czar Wants to Sleep*. [Translator.]

back to Russia and I never had anything more from him. Two or three times—I hope he was told—I passed on a friendly message to him. One day I met one of the leaders of Soviet music in Brussels where he happened to be at the time. I said to him: "Listen, since you're so kind to me, I'm going to ask you to do something for me. See Prokofiev and tell him I'm still fond of him, I still admire him." Did he pass on the message? I haven't a clue . . .

7

MAURICE RAVEL

Stéphane Audel. You'll accuse me of lacking imagination, but since we're to talk today about Maurice Ravel, and we have to begin at the beginning and ask you the question as hackneyed as it's customary: when did you first know the composer of *L'Enfant et les sortilèges?*

Francis Poulenc. I first knew him in March, 1917, very precisely. As I told you when I spoke to you about Honegger, at that time I was a piano pupil of Ricardo Viñes, and I spent my life in his house. You know that this musician, this wonderful pianist, who gave the first performances of most of Debussy's and Ravel's works, was remarkably cultured, and my piano lessons, which should have lasted an hour, sometimes used to last for two hours, two and a half, three hours because he'd read me a poem by Mallarmé, a page of Léon Bloy, or something by Huysmans, and while I was working with him I had a great desire one day to know Ravel. I was eighteen years old at the time, and as Ravel had been called up and later fallen ill, I'd never met him. Viñes said to me: "Listen, the best way . . . I'll ask Ravel for an appointment." Ravel was his close friend. "You can go and see him in the morning, show him your music and also play him the Sonatine you want to." I remember . . . I wanted to play him the "Forlane," the "Menuet" and the "Rigaudon" from *Le Tombeau de Couperin,* too. I "was" to play to him . . . because he only let me play for three minutes . . . Perhaps he thought

My Friends and Myself

I played badly, anyway, and immediately the conversation turned to music. I'd shown him some harmless piano pieces which he looked at with a severe eye, but nice all the same, and then we talked of one thing and another. At the time he lived in a flat in the avenue Mac-Mahon, at the Étoile . . .

S.A. What impression did you take away of your first interview with him?

F.P. Ah, there, there! An *awful* sense of disappointment.

S.A. No?

F.P. Yes, because Ravel was paradox itself, and I think that, in front of a young musician, he redoubled his paradoxical side . . . So, he explained to me that Schumann . . . pooh! pooh! pooh! . . . was a nonentity . . . that Mendelssohn . . . was wonderful . . . that Mendelssohn's *Songs Without Words* were a thousand times better than Schumann's *Carnaval*, that all the later works of Debussy—whom I worshipped—that is, *Jeux*, the *Études pour piano* . . . were none of them "good" Debussy. That Debussy's musical old age wasn't up to much; that Saint-Saëns was a musician of genius . . . that Chabrier wasn't equal to orchestrating his own music, and so on. All this bowled me over. I came out of it as if I'd been K.O.'d . . . He wasn't at all the musician I'd counted on seeing, and I must say it explains why, afterwards, Satie said to me—and here I have to use a crude word—"Everything that c— Ravel says is stupid." At that moment I naturally adopted the attitude of Satie and Auric, in other words a basically anti-Ravel attitude.

S.A. But tell me, there were pieces by Ravel that you admired all the same, others you admired less. Which are they?

F.P. Yes, naturally . . . there were some I admired . . . and now, my opinion is quite different from what it was at the time. However, there was a work I loathed, and that was *Le Tombeau de Couperin*.

Maurice Ravel

S.A. Loathed?

F.P. Violently!!! And I didn't like *Daphnis et Chloé* . . . Of course, you know, that was the time when Diaghilev was urging the young to disown their predecessors, their elders. And so, when we went to the Russian Ballet in Monte Carlo and they gave *Daphnis et Chloé* or even Falla's *El sombrero de tres picos* in the evening, Diaghilev would say: "You're going to hear that old music? Can you still listen to it . . . how boring! how terribly boring!!! . . ." It was a good thing, however, because that's how Diaghilev always made progress, by disowning what he'd loved, and basically the young ought to be like that. I *dote* on people who insult me, the twelve-note composers who find my music abominable. That's how it ought to be . . .

S.A. You're quite right, but in fact didn't your admiration for Satie and your stubbornness over Ravel bring about a coolness between you? Didn't you quarrel with Ravel?

F.P. I didn't quarrel but I no longer wanted to see him . . . I didn't see him for years . . . When I say I didn't see him . . . I'd bump into him in a concert hall, greet him and say hello to him . . . That's all. There was no intimacy. Until the time of *L'Enfant et les sortilèges*, when it was given at Monte Carlo . . . that was in 1925. Auric and I were there and we loved *L'Enfant et les sortilèges*. We made our peace with Ravel, and he thanked us for having been anti-Ravel, because he'd had enough of people copying him . . . And from 1925 until his death was perhaps the time when I was closest to him.

S.A. What were relations like between Stravinsky and Ravel?

F.P. Now that's very complicated! You know that Stravinsky and Ravel had been very close, and that in 1913, I think, Ravel had been living in Switzerland, at Morges, near Stravinsky's place, because he was re-orchestrating the lost passages from *Khovanshchina* for Diaghilev. There they were extremely close for a time, and it was then that Stravinsky composed the *Three Japanese Lyrics* and Ravel composed his *Trois poèmes de Stéphane Mallarmé* for the same combination of instruments. They dedicated one of their three songs to each other. Then, after that, there was a very great coolness between them that lasted, I should say, until Ravel's death. Ravel was a man very honest with himself, very uncompromising, and, from *Les Noces* onwards . . . he no longer liked Stravinsky's music . . . He didn't like *Oedipus Rex*, he liked nothing about it at all. And so, obviously, they never saw each other again, ever, ever, ever. I was present at a remarkable scene, a historic scene. It was in the house of a friend of Diaghilev's, Madame Missia Sert, who was painted by Toulouse-Lautrec, Bonnard, Renoir, was Mallarmé's friend, everybody's friend, and was Diaghilev's Muse . . . At Missia Sert's then, I was there when Ravel presented his *La Valse* to Diaghilev. There were very few people there . . . Diaghilev himself, Leonide Massine, Stravinsky, two or three of Diaghilev's secretaries . . . me . . . and Marcelle Meyer. Ravel arrived and played *La Valse* to Diaghilev.

S.A. At the piano?

F.P. At the piano. Diaghilev was to produce *La Valse* at the Russian Ballet with scenery by José-Maria Sert, who was Missia's husband. Ravel arrived without any fuss, his music under his arm, and Diaghilev said to him: "Well now . . .," (in that nasal voice of his, in fact mine is very good for imitating him), "well, my dear Ravel, what luck to hear *La Valse*! . . ." And Ravel played *La Valse*, with Marcelle Meyer, I think, perhaps not very well . . . but all the same it was *La Valse* by Ravel. Now, I knew Diaghilev very well at that time, and I'd seen his false teeth shift, his monocle move, I'd seen that he was very embarrassed, I'd seen that he didn't like it, I'd seen that he was about to say . . . "No." When Ravel

Maurice Ravel

finished, Diaghilev made a remark to him that I thought was very accurate: "Ravel, it's a masterpiece . . . but it's not a ballet . . . It's a portrait of a ballet . . . a painting of a ballet."

S.A. Wonderful!

F.P. And I think that's the reason why *La Valse* has never been a success from the point of view of the choreography. But the extraordinary thing about it is that Stravinsky said NOT ONE WORD!

S.A. Nothing at all?

F.P. Nothing. Now, this was in 1921, I was twenty-two, and I was dumbfounded, do you understand? And it gave me the lesson of a lifetime in modesty, because Ravel picked up his music very calmly, without worrying about what people thought, and went off again quite quietly. There, that explains the Ravel-Stravinsky, Stravinsky-Ravel situation.

S.A. Perfectly. That puts it in a . . . a quite dazzling light, I must say. Tell me, let's venture on a rather lighter, rather more superficial subject, shall we? Tristan Klingsor and Marguerite Long have both talked to me about Ravel. They told me—I think it had an important place in his life—about Ravel's elegance and dandyism.

F.P. Ah yes, it's quite remarkable. Stravinsky was always concerned about elegance, well-cut suits, high quality tweed, but through a kind of taste for luxury . . . Whereas it wasn't the quality of the material that counted for Ravel, it was the cut, often unusual, of the garment. I've a splendid photograph of Ravel. He is coming out of the "Grand Écart", which was famous at the time, with Léon-Paul Fargue, Paul Morand and Georges Auric. He looks dressed up like a little jockey. He's wearing a gabardine overcoat, a bowler hat, a dinner jacket and patent leather shoes! You don't know whether it's night or day. He set g*rrr*eat store on all that sort of thing. One day, when he was being congratulated at one of his concerts and a friend was shouting "Bravo, Ravel, it's magnificent!" he said to him: "Haven't you noticed I'm launching the bluebottle-green dinner jacket this evening?" Ha! there's a wonderful story Cocteau told me . . . a story about gloves. You remember that before 1914 men used to wear dress gloves with the facings turned back on their hands?

S.A. Yes, turned back on the upper part of the hand.

F.P. And, naturally, the dyers took a delight in stamping their marks on these facings . . .

S.A. On the inner facings, yes . . .

F.P. It was when Stravinsky and Ravel, after coming out from a rehearsal of *Daphnis et Chloé* in the Théâtre du Châtelet—that is, before 1914—were sitting at a table in the sun. They were drinking apéritifs and Stravinsky was looking at Ravel's gloves. Ravel said: "You're looking at my gloves?" "Yes," said Stravinsky, "they aren't new, are they?" And Ravel replied, "No, they're not . . . Don't you think they're nice?" "Yes," said Stravinsky with that sort of obsessional precision he's always shown when passing a judgement, "but what surprises me is that you haven't any dyer's marks. Have your gloves been to the dyer?" "Of course," said Ravel, a bit put out. "Well then, how do you manage it?" And at that moment Ravel turned his glove back completely and the dyer's marks were inside the fingers. He then said this, which is delightful: "What do you expect? We economical dandies!!!" Jean Cocteau was with them, in front of a glass of beer or an apéritif, and he's the one who told me the story.

S.A. It's charming: "economical dandies". But tell me, Ravel had many friends to whom he was attached, because he had a feeling for friendship, didn't he?

Maurice Ravel

F.P. Yes, he did, in an excellent sort of way, because Ravel was a living paradox. This man who wanted to seem harsh was in fact a man of tenderness, deep tenderness.

S.A. He was reserved, perhaps.

F.P. Ravel's life was bound up with his mother. The child in L'*Enfant et les sortilèges* is basically Ravel, the child who cries "Maman" and holds out its arms. He worshipped his mother. He was desperately sad when she died; and note this, he had no love-life to be spoken of; no one knows of any Ravel love affair. What he liked was friendship above all. I remember one evening in particular. There was a very brilliant *salon* at the time in Paris, the Godebski *salon*. Godebski was a great friend of Toulouse-Lautrec and the brother of Missia Sert I spoke to you about just now. Of course, they entertained a lot and their guests were among the top people. Gide used to come, and Fargue, Manuel de Falla, Stravinsky when he was in Paris, Bonnard, and Vuillard, too. A very brilliant gathering. Ravel came very often on Sundays. I can't say every Sunday, but very often, and it was for Godebski's children, in fact, that he wrote Ma Mère l'*Oye* for four hands. I was saying, then, that Ravel used to come there nearly every Sunday, and one day he asked: "Isn't Fargue here?" He was told: "No, Fargue won't be coming this evening." Whereupon he pouted like a disappointed child—for there was a childish side to the man, though in everything else he was tremendously sophisticated. Suddenly, contrary to what was thought, Fargue arrived at one o'clock in the morning. I'd like you to have heard the tone of voice in which Ravel cried out: "Ah, Fargue . . ." It was touching.

S.A. He had need of friendship. Tell me, did Ravel judge his own music clearly?

F.P. Oh, *fan-tast-ically* so! I'll tell you a story. One of the last occasions he conducted in public was in the Théâtre du

My Friends and Myself

Châtelet at a Colonne Concert. He conducted his *Rapsodie espagnole*. Now I've a very touching memory of this. He gave me the score he conducted from, perhaps as a conclusive sign of peace. Do you understand?

S.A. Yes, perfectly, like a peace pact.

F.P. And I told him how, each time I heard the *Rapsodie espagnole*—it had resisted my period of anti-Ravel bad temper —I was always astonished by it. "Yes, yes, the *Rapsodie espagnole*," he replied, "but the *Habanera*'s bungled!" "What? The *Habanera*'s bungled?" "Yes, yes, the *Habanera* doesn't come off . . ." I went on: "I know why you say that, Ravel. It's because it was originally a piece for two pianos which you orchestrated and slipped into the *Rapsodie espagnole*, and that's the only reason." He insisted: "No, no, I like the music, but it's so badly orchestrated!!!" I protested: "How can you claim that the *Habanera* is badly orchestrated?"

S.A. Imagine *him* saying that!!

F.P. Then he made this excellent remark to me, the remark of a truly extraordinary technician: "There's too much orchestration for the number of bars." It's an astonishing remark. By an astonishing technician. He also said to Auric: "I'd like you to help me . . . I'd like to write a treatise on orchestration on the lines of Rimsky-Korsakov's with little examples taken from my music, except that they'd show *what not to do* . . . *what I've bungled!!!*" By contrast with Rimsky, who set himself up as an example.

S.A. It proves his very great modesty.

F.P. He was remarkably modest.

S.A. Did you go on seeing Ravel until the end of his life?

F.P. Yes, a lot, a lot, and it was during that period, perhaps, that I loved him, as I did Honegger. It's odd, but that's how things happen. I can remember something very moving. On one of the last occasions when Ravel went out, he came to a concert I was giving with Pierre Bernac, and Pierre sang Ravel's *Histoires naturelles* with me accompanying. That was also the day we'd given the first performance of my song cycle, *Tel jour, telle nuit*. I must say Ravel had been touching in his kindness both to the accompanist of his music and to the composer, but I remember that at the time he was unable to find the words he wanted. Up to the end, however, he remained wonderfully lucid about his craft. One day Madeleine Grey and I were rehearsing for a performance of his *Don Quichotte à Dulcinée* songs . . . and I'd said to Madeleine Grey that perhaps Ravel would like to come. And Ravel, in fact, did come with his brother. He was almost in a coma at the time, I must say, and Madeleine Grey, who was an excellent singer but very wayward, said: "One of the notes is giving me trouble . . . I'll sing it as a dotted note, Ravel won't notice."

S.A. And she dotted it?

F.P. She did. I said: "All right, Madeleine, but it may be dangerous." "No it won't," she said, "he won't notice." Whereupon Ravel arrived, I tell you, in a state of mental coma. He sat down in a chair and we played the piece. "Ah," he said, "that was very good, very good." "But there's something about it you don't like, Ravel," I said. "I can see it in your look. What is it? Is it too fast? Is it too loud? Is it too . . . ?" Since he didn't speak, I insisted: "Please, please. We're here to rehearse with you, say anything!" And then he got up from his chair and went to the piano—without saying a word —and put his finger on the note Madeleine Grey had dotted, and, like a child, (it was horrible, painful indeed . . .) he said: "There!" and he was pointing to THE NOTE!!!

S.A. The very note! It proves he'd retained great lucidity, nonetheless.

My Friends and Myself

F.P. It's odd. This character, this character who was, I've told you, dressed so strangely, this paradoxical character, well, it was illness that made him human and, for me, left an impression that was, on the contrary, very lyrical . . . it's odd and it's moving.

8

IGOR STRAVINSKY

Stéphane Audel. Igor Stravinsky has just celebrated his eightieth birthday. I know you have a deep admiration for the composer of *Le Sacre du printemps*. When does it date from?

Francis Poulenc. Good Lord! I'm sixty-three now and my admiration for Stravinsky dates from when I was eleven! That's how old I was when I had the luck to hear some of Stravinsky's music for the first time. I think, if memory is correct, that it was at one of the Colonne Concerts; Gabriel Pierné was conducting. Let's see . . . I remember now . . . He conducted *Feux d'artifice* and the *Berceuse* from *L'Oiseau de feu*. It was a number he conducted very often, wonderfully in fact, all the more so in that he was the man who conducted *L'Oiseau de feu* for the first time with Diaghilev's Russian Ballet. Notice that I knew a lot of contemporary music at that time; I worshipped Debussy, who's always been a religion with me, but the SOUND of Stravinsky's music was something so new to me that I often ask myself: "Well, if Stravinsky had never existed, would I have written music?" Which means to say that I consider myself as a son, the type of son he could certainly disown, but in fact a spiritual son of Stravinsky. I was brought up very liberally, and, thank Heaven, my family let me go to the theatre and the ballet when I was very young. That's how I was able to hear *Le Sacre du printemps* in 1913 at the Théâtre des Champs-Élysées. The choreography fascinated me, as did the music. The following winter I took part in the battle of *Le Sacre du printemps* conducted by Monteux at a concert in the Casino de Paris. The odd thing about it is—and I often ask myself the question—why wasn't I influenced by *Le Sacre du printemps*, when I'd been influenced by so many other of Stravinsky's works? When I heard *Le Sacre du printemps* I was, of course, very young, since it was in 1913 and I was fourteen. But obviously it was a revolution as far as I was concerned, and a revolution from every point of view, because Nijinsky's choreography had overwhelmed me. As a matter of fact, people are unfair to Nijinsky, they always talk about the dancer and too often forget the utterly inspired choreographer he was. You can imagine what a state I was in when I came out of the Théâtre des Champs-Élysées after the performance of the ballet, and what I was like coming out of the Casino de Paris where, the following winter, Monteux conducted *Le Sacre du printemps* at a Sunday concert. The work had been a shock to me such as I'd dreamed about, such a shock, in fact, that I tried—I still didn't have the score—I tried to remember at the piano those strange and dissonant chords. Anyway, I got hold of the music very quickly afterwards and spent my time playing it in four-handed arrangements, because at that time there were no gramophone records unfortunately, and four-handed arrangements, as well as music for two pianos, provided the only way to remember things. I got a fantastic shock . . . a *fan-tast-ic shock*, but it wasn't *Le Sacre du printemps* that influenced me. I was influenced by works that are much more European like *Pulcinella, Le Baiser de la fée, Jeu de cartes, Mavra* . . . d'you see?

S.A. Perfectly. But that extraordinary shock you experienced, like many other musicians in fact, one might say all the musicians of your generation . . .

Igor Stravinsky

F.P. All musicians, certainly.

S.A. As far as you're concerned, it's odd to see that *Le Sacre du printemps* hasn't influenced you at all.

F.P. No, no, no.

S.A. While everyone else, on the contrary, fell under the spell in some way. All the same, given your admiration for Stravinsky, I assume you had a very keen desire to meet him?

F.P. Naturally. You can imagine ! ! ! But I only knew Stravinsky when I was a bit older. I saw him in 1916, when, for the first time during the war, he came back from Switzerland. I met him quite by chance at my publisher's, and when I saw him come in I thought it was God Himself making an entrance. Really! By a remarkable bit of luck I had the four-handed arrangement of *Petrouchka* with me and I asked him to write a few words in it. That was the first contact I had with him. Now on that occasion I hadn't said half a dozen words, but next winter, on his return in 1917 for Diaghilev's season when *Parade* had its first performance, I saw a lot of him. From that time onwards I'm proud to say I've been his friend, one of his friends, in fact.

S.A. And his interpreter, I think?

F.P. And also his interpreter, because I still say it was a great honour for me to have played one of the four pianos in *Les Noces*. I was to have taken part at the first performance in 1923, but unfortunately I was prevented at the last moment because I had an unlucky attack of jaundice. But immediately after the first series of performances I was at my piano again, and I must say that I played *Les Noces* more than forty times. With, moreover, a conductor who conducts it better than anyone else—Ansermet.

S.A. He's unrivalled for Stravinsky.

F.P. I even played *Les Noces* with Stravinsky and a vast

number of conductors, in London, Paris, Switzerland, Italy, Spain, and the remarkable thing is that with Ansermet it's easy to play.

S.A. Who were the other pianists, because there were four, weren't there?

F.P. Yes. At the first performance the pianists were: Marcelle Meyer, the great pianist who's now unfortunately dead, Hélène Léon who's dead too, Georges Auric and me. That was to have been the team for the première. Since I was ill, a conductor from Monte Carlo called Flamand played the fourth piano.

S.A. Tell me, Francis, what were your relations with Stravinsky like? Were they easy, friendly, pleasant?

F.P. Very easy. He was extremely good to me, because, remember, it was Stravinsky who got me published in London —by Chester's, my first publishers, the publishers of *Mouvements perpétuels,* my Sonata for two clarinets, my Sonata for four hands. All those beginners' pieces, stammering little pieces, were published thanks to Stravinsky's kindness. He was really a father to me. I lived on very close terms with him until life separated us. He lives in America and I see him very rarely now, but my feelings towards him remain exactly the same, they're even warmer, and I've unending admiration for him. On the whole I like all the periods he's been through. There are some that are closer to me, but even his last period, which is very far removed from me, I deeply admire. I admire a man who can renew himself at the age of seventy-five, it's a wonderful thing, even if he distils his honey from other people's discoveries; Schoenberg's, Webern's. In fact, it's an excellent thing that Stravinsky . . . Look, it's like Picasso, they're people who make their honey . . .

S.A. Without a doubt, but if you don't mind we'll come back in a minute to that astonishing link between Picasso and

Igor Stravinsky

Stravinsky. For the time being I'd like to ask you a question. Since you refer to the variety of the great Igor's work, I'd like to ask you this: Take L'Histoire du soldat which he wrote at Morges during the 1914 war to words by Ramuz, with whom he was very friendly and who also lived at Morges. Do you think this particular work can be seen as a turning point in Stravinsky's output?

F.P. It's a major work! To begin with, it's an outstanding work, and then you can date it easily. It belongs very precisely to the period. When you hear L'Histoire du soldat you know very well that it hovers around the years 1916, 1917, 1918 ... It's vital. Because from that time onwards Stravinsky left behind what's called his truly Russian period; after Les Noces, after Renard ... I love L'Histoire du soldat, I think it's a remarkable work, and really, I assure you, it's the key in the lock for everything that's about to follow.

S.A. So it's a turning point.

F.P. A decisive turning point. It's very, very important.

S.A. You referred earlier to Debussy's wide culture, and when you spoke of cultured musicians in our conversation about Ravel you told me that Stravinsky was a man of vast culture and that in his everyday conversation he drew on superior powers of argument. I wonder to what point this vast culture has contributed to the many-sided aspect of his work?

F.P. No, no. Stravinsky's culture is in direct relation to what he's doing at the moment. For example: he decides to compose an opera. Right. So then he educates himself in the meaning of the opera as well as from the point of view of the libretto. Suddenly Stravinsky interests himself in da Ponte ... you see what I mean, don't you? It's always related to what he's doing, because with Stravinsky there's such a concern for precision that he likes to find the equivalent in another art of what he's looking for himself. One day I arrived at his home

My Friends and Myself

at the time when he was writing *Apollon Musagète*. He'd discovered—and this is very droll—he'd discovered . . . Boileau, the classical poet! Boileau the poet! Suddenly he thought Boileau was a wonderful poet. He said to me: "Do you like Boileau?" I said: "Yes . . . though not to extremes. Not like Racine." He said: "It's wonderful! I've just found a line in Boileau's *L'Art poétique* which is exactly what I needed to put as a motto for a variation for one of my Muses." In fact, that line of Boileau's is featured in the published score, though I'm incapable of quoting it to you. It's a didactic line pointing out that the length of a line ought to be . . . you see what I mean? So that did duty for what Stravinsky was after. Debussy had a culture which was useful to him, because the very fact of improving one's mind brings about enrichment, but Debussy's was in all directions, whereas Stravinsky follows a straight line. For example, when he wrote all his latest works. At the time he began to re-consider composers he'd perhaps neglected until then, such as Heinrich Isaac, and the German and Dutch contrapuntists . . . When you enter Stravinsky's home and see the music he's got on his piano and on his table, you can guess pretty well what he's writing.

S.A. What he's writing at the moment?

F.P. Yes. When I went to see him—I think it was in 1940, no, it was 1949—when I went to see him in Hollywood and walked into his studio, I spied Mozart scores, Rossini scores, Bellini scores . . . He was writing *The Rake's Progress*.

S.A. *The Rake's Progress* is steeped in Mozart, with sauce à la Stravinsky, of course.

F.P. Stravinsky is versatile, of course, but the thing to admire about him is that he's Stravinsky above everything else.

S.A. Yes, that's what's extraordinary.

Igor Stravinsky

F.P. In those recent twelve-note things he wrote, you said to yourself: "Well, well, well! Is this by Stravinsky? ..." And suddenly there's a chord, an orchestral sound ...

S.A. And you can doubt no longer ... it's Stravinsky!

F.P. Two bars ... and everything he adopts he makes his own.

S.A. It's the characteristic of a genius to take his inspiration where he finds it.

F.P. Stravinsky has every type of genius because he has the genius of invention, of form and of colour. It's really astonishing. And when you re-hear some of his works you'd thought you liked less, the Violin Concerto, for example, which I thought I didn't like much ... Well, I heard it on the radio by chance the other day. Yes, that's one of radio's benefits. And I thought: "It's a wonderful Violin Concerto!" Of course, it's not one of Stravinsky's works I prefer, but when you hear it independently, isolated, you say to yourself: "How lovely it is!"

S.A. That's how you can recognize genius ... Since we're talking of Stravinsky's genius, it's beyond doubt that he's both an example and a warning, because, in fact, the people who follow him too closely, the less distinguished second generation, are the living dead.

F.P. That's the case with all great composers ... It's the case with Debussy, it's the case with Schoenberg, with Webern ...

S.A. They're people who are very widely imitated ... Whereas they're inimitable!

F.P. Exactly, that's it exactly. Only the splendid thing about Stravinsky is that his material is so rich that it can serve as leaven for the young. And that's what the chaps of my generation had the luck to get. He was a stimulus; it was genuine

My Friends and Myself

leaven, while on the other hand there are composers, notable ones perhaps, but who don't bring about . . .

S.A. Who don't bring about any reaction, any call, and who enrich no one. Since we're talking about this very subject, let's trace a parallel that's often drawn; it's become almost a commonplace to read it, but it's certain that there's a relationship from the point of view of talent, genius, curiosity, culture and also tremendous knowledge of their craft, between Picasso and Stravinsky.

F.P. Yes, certainly. They definitely have many things in common, if only that versatile genius which results in Stravinsky always being Stravinsky and Picasso always being Picasso, but nevertheless there is one great difference; and I'll make a remark that takes nothing away from Stravinsky's stature. His old age is a restless one, in other words, at the age of seventy-five he says to himself: "Doesn't my path lie in composing twelve-note music?" Whereas Picasso's old age is serene. In fact, Picasso . . . couldn't give a damn about anything.

S.A. He enjoys himself.

F.P. He enjoys himself. He knows he's a BIG SHOT and that everybody will copy him. He's not afraid of the young, d'you see?

S.A. Exactly. Anyway, he's exhausted all the different techniques . . . he can do a drawing as perfect as those by Ingres . . .

F.P. Stravinsky too! Stravinsky can orchestrate Pergolesi . . .

S.A. And has done.

F.P. He can give rebirth to Tchaikovsky themes. I'm talking to you about all this very informally. You mustn't expect to see me talking as if I were giving a lecture on "the work of Stravinsky". It's precisely because I worship him, because I admire him, because I'm often sad at no longer seeing him,

Igor Stravinsky

that I'm talking in fits and starts. That's what it is, I think, that gives warmth to my admiration and that's what I wanted. Just imagine that at this moment you're in my room, in my study, and that you arrive and find on my piano all of Stravinsky's music, all his records on my gramophone, and you say: "Well, you really like him!" And I declare: "I WORRRSHIP HIM!"

Personalia

Apollinaire, Guillaume, (Kostrowitzky), 1880-1918. One of the greatest of modern French poets. His work has a unique combination of nostalgia and melancholy. *Les Mamelles de Tirésias* is an early example of Surrealism in the theatre.

Aragon, Louis, b.1897. Communist poet and novelist, prominent in the Dada and Surrealist movements of the twenties. Now a member of that highly respectable literary establishment the Académie Goncourt.

Auric, Georges, b.1899. The youngest member of *Les Six*. Has composed a great deal for ballet, film and stage, as well as writing quantities of songs, piano and symphonic works.

Boileau, Nicolas, 1636-1711. Critic and satirical poet, especially remembered for his insistence on the classical rules of composition.

Breton, André, 1896-1967. Poet and chief exponent of Surrealism, notably with the *Manifeste du surréalisme*, 1924. His book, *Nadja*, 1928, applies Surrealist doctrine to the novel, and his poetry derives from Freud, Rimbaud, Lautréamont and the German Romantics.

Caplet, André, 1878-1925. Composer and conductor, friend of Debussy.

Casella, Alfredo, 1883-1947. Italian composer and pianist, influenced by French music, who was a pupil of Fauré.

Cendrars, Blaise, (Frédéric Sauser), 1887-1961. Swiss poet, novelist and critic in the vanguard of most modern French literary movements. His multitudinous work is largely in-inspired by his own far-ranging travels throughout the world.

Clair, René, (Chomette), b.1898. Director of French films, many of them classics, from the twenties onwards. Also an entertaining writer of novels as well as film scripts.

Copeau, Jacques, 1879-1949. Actor, producer, and director of the experimental Théâtre du Vieux-Colombier.

Crevel, René, 1900-1935. Surrealist poet.

Cousin, Victor, 1792-1867. Philosopher.

Daumier, Honoré, 1808-1879. Lithographer and caricaturist renowned for his caustic satire.

Desnos, Robert, 1900-1945. Surrealist poet who later left the movement to go his own way with poems of a light simplicity.

Dullin, Charles, 1885-1949. Actor, producer, and founder of the pioneer Théâtre de l'Atelier.

Durey, Louis, b.1888. Member of *Les Six,* though not associated with them for long. Wrote chamber music, songs, etc., and then became deeply interested in Communism.

Fargue, Léon-Paul, 1876-1947. Poet who wrote at length about Paris, its sights, sounds and inhabitants.

Gédalge, André, 1856-1926. Composer of symphonic and stage works, but best known as a brilliant teacher of fugue and counterpoint at the Conservatoire.

Jouvet, Louis, 1887-1951. Actor and Producer.

Klingsor, Tristan, (Leon Leclère), 1874-1966. Poet, artist and occasional composer, whence the Wagnerian pseudonym.

Koechlin, Charles, 1867-1950. Prolific composer in many genres. His great erudition and genuine sympathy with youth made him an excellent teacher.

Personalia

Larbaud, Valéry, 1881-1957. Novelist and translator into French of James Joyce and Samuel Butler.

Mendès, Catulle, 1842-1909. Long-forgotten versifier and journalist.

Milhaud, Darius, b.1892. Member of Les Six. A disconcertingly prolific composer of songs, choral music, symphonic works, concertos, oratorios, operas, ballets and stage and film music.

Mompou, Frederico, b.1893. Spanish composer who had his early successes in France with austere but lyrical works.

Morand, Paul, b.1888. Poet and novelist, very much a twenties figure, though as active as ever.

Pedrell, Felipe, 1841-1922. Spanish composer and musicologist. His music is based on traditional themes, but he has had most influence as editor and re-discoverer of his country's music.

Pierné, Gabriel, 1863-1937. Composer of operas, ballets, oratorios, symphonic works, etc., and a famous conductor in his time.

Polignac, Princesse Edmond de, (Wennaretta Singer), 1865-1943. American-born patroness of the arts and a generous supporter of many contemporary composers.

Pougy, Liane de, later Princesse Ghyka, died 1949. Notorious cocotte of the nineteen-hundreds.

Radiguet, Raymond, 1903-1923. A protégé of Jean Cocteau, he was a precociously gifted novelist whose *Le Diable au corps* and *Le Bal du comte d'Orgel* are classics of modern French literature.

Ramuz, Louis-Ferdinand, 1878-1947. Prolific Swiss writer of novels which are generally set in the Vaudois and Valais Alps.

Reverdy, Pierre, 1889-1960. Poet and forerunner of the Surrealists, with whom he had much in common.

My Friends and Myself

Roland-Manuel, Alexis, 1891-1966. Composer, musicologist and critic.

Roussel, Albert, 1869-1937. Sailor turned composer—symphonies, ballets (*Le Festin de l'araignée*), and much else that has given him an important position in contemporary French music.

Samain, Albert, 1858-1900. Symbolist poet, author of delicate and impressionistic verse.

Sauguet, Henri, b.1901. Gifted composer for the theatre—ballets, operas and incidental film music—and a quantity of vocal works.

Schmitt, Florent, 1870-1958. A formidable composer alternating between ambitious Wagnerian romanticism and passages of humour.

Tailleferre, Germaine, b.1892. Only woman member of *Les Six*, she has written chamber music, ballets, opéras-comiques, and has set Valéry's *Narcisse*.

Thibaud, Jacques, 1880-1953. Distinguished French violinist and a superb player of his own country's music.

Vidal, Paul, 1863-1931. Composer, conductor, and teacher of composition at the Conservatoire.

Index

Aguet, William, 110
Albéniz, Isaac, 89, 93, 94
Albert-Ribot, Germaine, 54
Ansermet, Ernest, 137, 138
Apollinaire, Guillaume, 41, 51–2, 54, 55, 59, 68, 73, 74, 84, 98, 99, 100, 102, 145
Aragon, Louis, 49, 98, 99, 101, 145
Auric, Georges, 21, 39, 40, 41, 42, 43, 64, 66, 68, 70, 76, 83, 108, 109, 117, 119, 127, 129, 132, 138, 145
Avila, St. Teresa of, 87–8

Bach, Johann Sebastian, 35, 47
Balguerie, Suzanne, 69
Balzac, Honoré de, 32, 117
Bartók, Béla, 14, 23, 24, 34, 48, 58, 90, 93
Basil, Colonel de, 117
Bathori, Jane, 40–1, 45, 69, 106, 107
Baudelaire, Charles Pierre, 48, 59, 73, 102
Beethoven, Ludwig van, 30, 58, 113
Bellini, Vincenzo, 140
Berg, Alban, 13, 59, 118
Berlioz, Hector, 30, 113
Bernas, Pierre, 45, 47, 48, 49, 50, 133
Bloy, Léon, 125
Boileau, Nicolas, 14, 145
Boulez, Pierre, 22

Braque, Georges, 42, 43, 58, 69, 70, 73, 75, 98
Breton, André, 69, 84, 98, 99, 100, 101, 145
Brianchon, Maurice, 52, 58
Bullin, Charles, 41

Caplet, André, 106, 145
Casella, Alfredo, 38, 120, 145
Cendrars, Blaise, 98, 145
Chabrier, Emmanuel, 14, 48, 54, 58, 65, 88, 126
Chaliapin, Feodor, 115
Charpentier, Marc-Antoine, 113
Chevalier, Yvonne, 88
Chopin, Frédéric, 29, 30, 37, 58, 59
Clair, René, 24, 146
Claudel, Paul, 42, 69, 70, 98, 110
Clément, Edmont, 33
Cocteau, Jean, 21, 22, 42, 43, 58, 66, 68, 70, 84, 98, 108, 130
Colle, Pierre, 83
Collet, Henri, 108
Coolidge, Mrs, 116
Couperin, François, 31, 46
Cousin, Victor, 69, 146

Dali, Salvador, 101, 105
Danco, Suzanne, 69
Daudet family, 76
Debussy, Claude, 14, 34, 36, 37, 39, 41, 47, 48, 58, 59, 60, 63, 64, 65, 92, 93, 106, 121, 125, 126, 135, 139, 140, 141

Index

Defauw, Désiré, 53
Derain, André, 69, 75, 83, 98
Déroulède, Paul, 104
Diaghilev, Serge, 13, 21, 39, 43, 44, 67, 68, 92, 109, 114, 127, 128, 135, 137
Diderot, Denis, 35, 46
Dufy, Raoul, 51, 58
Dukas, Paul, 40, 42, 113
Duparc, Henri, 48
Durey, Louis, 41, 42, 68, 146
Duval, Denise, 24, 55

Eisenstein, Sergei, 121, 123
Éluard, Paul, 21, 45, 49-50, 51, 57, 59, 84, 97-105
Ernst, Max, 101

Falla, Manuel de, 14, 45, 46, 63, 69, 87-96, 102, 131
Fargue, Léon-Paul, 37, 67, 69, 98, 129, 131, 146
Fauconnet, 108
Fauré, Gabriel, 48, 59, 88, 89, 113
Ferat, Serge, 54
Février, Jacques, 88, 116, 119
Franck, César, 30, 34
Franck, Yvonne, 85
Frescobaldi, Girolamo, 91
Freund, Marya, 22, 69

Gautier, Théophile, 102
Gédalge, André, 35, 146
Ghyka, Princesse, 73, 147
Gide, André, 69, 70, 98, 100, 117, 131
Gogh, Vincent van, 113
Gounod, Charles, 48
Goya, Francisco, 88
Grey, Madeleine, 133
Gris, Juan, 42, 75

Halffter, Ernesto, 96
Haydn, Josef, 58

Hindemith, Paul, 14, 23, 59, 64
Honegger, Arthur, 41, 42, 43, 64, 65, 106-13, 125, 132
Honegger, Mme, 106
Horowitz, Vladimir, 38, 53
Hugo, Jean, 108

Isaac, Heinrich, 140

Jacob, Max, 72-86, 87, 89, 98, 99, 102, 116
Jouvet, Louis, 41, 146
Joyce, James, 98

Karajan, Herbert von, 47
Koechlin, Charles, 35-8, 107, 146
Kokoschka, Oskar, 23
Koussevitzky, Serge, 122

La Fontaine, Jean de, 59, 103
Landowska, Wanda, 13, 21, 45, 94, 95, 96
Larbaud, Valéry, 98, 147
Laurencin, Marie, 43, 52
Léger, Fernand, 98, 109
Léon, Hélène, 138
Lifar, Serge, 47
Linossier, Raymonde, 98
Liszt, Franz, 29, 32

Mahler, Gustav, 14, 22
Mallarmé, Stéphane, 49, 102, 125
Mantegna, Andrea, 57, 58
Manuel, Claude, 121
Marcel, Gabriel, 46 fn. 1
Massenet, Jules, 30
Massine, Leonide, 114, 128
Matisse, Henri, 68, 73, 118
Mendelssohn, Felix, 126
Mendès, Catulle, 65, 147
Messager, André, 44
Meyer, Marcelle, 37, 128, 138
Milhaud, Darius, 22, 35, 36, 41,

150

Index

42, 59, 64, 70, 80, 107, 108, 109, 110, 147
Mitropoulos, Dimitri, 53
Modigliani, Amedeo, 42, 74, 75
Mompou, Frederico, 37, 147
Monnier, Adrienne, 69, 70, 98, 99, 100
Monteux, Pierre, 23, 136
Monteverdi, Claudio, 58
Monvel, Mlle de, 34
Morand, Paul, 22, 129, 147
Mozart, Wolfgang Amadeus, 29, 30, 58, 59, 140
Muccioli, M., 35
Mussorgsky, Modest, 14, 58, 117

Nemtchinova, 44
Nijinsky, 44, 136
Noailles, Vicomtesse de, 16, 21

Ortiz, 46

Pascal, Blaise, 76
Pedrell, Felipe, 89, 90, 147
Pergolesi, Giovanni Battista, 142
Picasso, Pablo, 39, 57, 58, 64, 68, 69, 70, 73, 74, 75, 84, 92, 105, 118, 138, 142
Pierné, Gabriel, 135, 147
Plato, 69
Polignac, Princesse de, 16, 21, 45, 53, 69, 88, 89, 94, 95, 147
Posel, Jacques, 76
Prés, Josquin des, 58
Prévost, Jacques, 73
Prokofiev, Serge, 14, 20, 109, 114–24
Proust, Marcel, 21, 77, 80, 98, 116, 117
Puccini, Giacomo, 14
Racine, Jean, 140
Radiguet, Raymond, 73, 74, 108, 147

Ravel, Maurice, 34, 36, 37, 41, 48, 51, 58, 63, 64, 67, 88, 92, 93, 95, 106, 107, 117, 125–34
Rimbaud, Jean, 49, 73, 102
Rimsky-Korsakov, Nikolai, 36, 132
Riss-Arbeau, Mme, 30
Roland-Manuel, Alexis, 68, 96, 148
Ronsard, Pierre de, 32, 59
Rossini, Gioacchino, 140
Rostand, Claude, 112 fn.1
Rouault, Georges, 117, 118
Rosseau, Jean-Jacques, 46
Roussel, Albert, 41, 59, 109, 148
Royer, Marcel, 20, 30
Rubinstein, Artur, 88, 89
Rubinstein, Ida, 109

Sacher, Paul, 110, 112
Saint-Saëns, Camille, 126
Salabert, Mme, 18
Samain, Albert, 48, 148
Satie, Erik, 21, 23, 37, 39, 43, 58, 87, 88, 102, 109, 113, 126, 127
Sauguet, Henri, 36, 64, 117, 119, 148
Scarlatti, Domenico, 58
Schmitt, Florent, 42, 92, 148
Schoenberg, Arnold, 13, 21, 22–3, 34, 118, 121, 138, 141
Schubert, Franz, 30, 58, 59, 121
Schumann, Robert, 29, 63, 113, 126
Sert, José-Maria, 85, 128
Sienkiewicz, Mme, 36
Soret, Cécile, 76, 80
Stauermann, Edward, 22
Strauss, Richard, 88, 113
Stravinsky, Igor, 14, 22, 24, 32, 33, 34, 36, 43, 46, 48, 58, 59, 60, 63, 64, 67, 69, 88, 109, 114, 117, 119, 127, 128, 129, 130, 131, 135–43

Index

Tailleferre, Germaine de, 41, 42, 68, 108, 148
Tchaikovsky, Peter Ilich, 142
Thibaud, Jacques, 20, 148
Tolstoy, Leo, 121
Toulouse-Lautrec, Henri de, 30

Valéry, Paul, 49, 51, 69, 70, 84, 98, 99
Verdi, Giuseppe, 14, 58
Verlaine, Paul, 49, 102
Vidal, Paul, 40, 148
Viñes, Ricardo, 36–8, 39, 45, 46, 63, 90, 91, 106, 125

Vlaminck, Maurice, 98
Vuillermoz, Émile, 54

Wagner, Erika, 22, 32
Wagner, Richard, 65, fn. 1, 108
Warlich, 47
Weber, Carl Maria von, 58
Webern, Anton, 13, 19, 22, 24, 59, 64, 68, 121, 138, 141

Zuloga, 88
Zurbaran, Francisco, 57, 58, 88